NOT AS CRAZY
AS I SEEM

NOT AS CRAZY AS I SEEM

george harrar

Houghton Mifflin Company
Boston 2003

www.houghtonmifflinbooks.com

The text of this book is set in Utopia.

Library of Congress Cataloging-in-Publication Data

Harrar, George.
Not as crazy as I seem / George Harrar.
p. cm.
Summary: As fifteen-year-old Devon begins midyear at a new prestigious prep
school, he is plagued by compulsions such as the need to sort things into
groups of four.
ISBN 0-618-26365-9 (hardcover)
[1. Obsessive-compulsive disorder—Fiction. 2. Death—Fiction.
3. Grandfathers—Fiction. 4. Funeral rites and ceremonies—Fiction.
5. High schools—Fiction. 6. Schools—Fiction. 7. Vandalism—Fiction.] I. Title.
PZ7.H2346 No 2003
[Fic]—dc21
2002011671

Manufactured in the United States of America
QUM 10 9 8 7 6 5 4 3 2 1

prologue

"Hello, Devon. I'm Dr. Wasserman."

The big, black-bearded shrink jabs his hand at me. His fingers look huge, like thick pink sausages.

"I just washed, Doc." I shake my hands in the air so he'll get the idea. "I'm still kind of wet."

"That's very thoughtful of you. Have a seat wherever you like."

He sweeps his hand across the room like there are a million choices. I see two—a black vinyl chair with a small rip in the cushion and a white couch with a few brown spots on the arm. You'd think a doctor charging a hundred dollars an hour could afford better furniture.

"Is something the matter?"

"I like standing. It's good for you."

"I suppose it is. So, you want to stand right there?"

Not here exactly. Not here at all. I'd rather be standing almost anywhere else in the whole universe. I back up a few steps. "Here, I think."

"Okay, well, I understand that you're fifteen years old, and your family recently moved to town from the western part of the state—Amherst, right?"

"Not Amherst really. More like greater Amherst, you know, like how they say 'greater Boston'?"

"Yes, I have heard that. And you've been in therapy before."

"Oh yeah, for five months and six days."

"Did you find it helpful?"

I wish all questions were either yes or no, then I could

nod or shake my head and not have to think any more about them. Was therapy helpful? That depends on what it was supposed to do for me. Make me normal like other people? I don't want to be like any other person I've ever met, especially the normal ones. Normal is boring. Normal is going through life half-asleep, never really seeing things. But that's not what a shrink wants to hear. "Maybe."

He lifts up a folder stuffed with papers. "Your last doctor sent me your file. Apparently he didn't complete his analysis before your family moved here, but the notes indicate you've been experiencing generalized anxiety. Does that sound right to you?"

The anxiety doesn't feel very generalized to me. I'm not anxious about *everything*. I'm not anxious about most things, in fact, if you count every little thing there is in the world. It's just some things, at certain times, in some places that scare me out of my skin.

CHAPTER 1

English, Algebra, Biology, Lunch, Free Period, Gym, Classics,
Done. EnglishAlgebraBiologyLunchFreePeriodGymClassics
Done. EnglishAlgebra . . .

A knock on my door interrupts the words flowing through
my brain. I can tell it's my mother—she always knocks
twice. She'll want to come all the way into my room. She
won't even ask.

"I'm naked, Mom."

"Just pull something around you."

I sit upright on my squeaky new bed with the new purple comforter she bought me. Purple doesn't seem comfortable to me. I'd rather have black—black sheets and
black pillowcases and a black comforter. Black doesn't
make you think of anything. Black doesn't keep you up at
night. Why don't they make black sheets? Kids would buy
a ton of them.

I'm not naked, but I grab a pillow to hold in front of me. With my mother it's always better to have something to hold on to.

She opens the door a little.

"I'm kind of busy, Mom." *EnglishAlgebraBiology* . . .

She slips into my room and looks around. "It's coming along. I like how you've arranged your things. It's nice to start over in a new place, isn't it?"

No. I liked my old room on the third floor of my last house, fourteen steps between me and the parents. Mom never just dropped in at my old room. She hates steps ever since she twisted her back playing tennis. Mom used to have a killer serve, but now she just taps the ball over the net. It's kind of sad to see.

She picks up one of my snow globes and shakes it. Silver snow falls on four tiny fiddlers in Nashville. Dad still brings me a globe every time he goes on a business trip. No CDs or T-shirts or video games—I get snow globes. I have fourteen of them. Actually, I think they're kind of cool.

Mom puts back the snow globe and stoops down to look at the paperbacks on my bottom shelf. She reads the titles out loud—*Rats, Lice, and History; Mushrooms, Molds, and Miracles; Satan, Sin, and Sacrifice*. "I don't remember buying these books for you."

What's she think, I'm still, like, ten years old, when I wouldn't go to a store without her? "I bought them myself, Mom, at Annie's."

Everything cost two bucks at Annie's Used Books in Amherst. Annie said I was her most regular customer. I went in every Friday after school and finished a book every weekend. That really isn't hard when you don't have anything else to do. I don't mean to sound like Poor Devon the Friendless. I could have made friends. I didn't try. Friends are a lot of work.

Mom opens my Chinese lacquer box, the one with the alien-looking butterflies on the lid, and then closes it again when she sees it's empty. She grabs a handful of my small white meditation stones from the straw basket on the bookshelf and massages her fingers with them.

"You want something, Carole?" I think it's funny when I use her first name. It makes me feel like I'm forty years old. She gives me one of her faster-than-the-speed-of-light fake smiles.

"I just thought we should talk, since tomorrow's your first day."

EnglishAlgebraBiologyLunchFreePeriodGymClassics Done.

"About what?"

She lets the stones drop through her fingers back into the basket. "Private school may be a little tougher for you. And starting midyear in a new place isn't easy. Don't put too much pressure on yourself. You don't need to get straight A's, you know. A B now and then wouldn't kill you."

How does she know that? Why are people always so sure bad things won't happen if you don't do everything exactly right?

She leans over my desk to look at the row of faces from the newspaper that I just taped to my wall, and I see the sharp angle of her breasts pressing out against her white blouse. I wonder if she leans over much in the courtroom, and do the jurors think she's hot?

"Who are these people, Devon?"

Weirdos, crazies, maniacs—all-American nuts, that's who. People who make the headlines. People who look like everyday goofy kids in their high school pictures, and then crazy mountain men when you see them in the papers twenty years later.

"Nobody special." I know she won't leave it at that. A lawyer never stops asking questions until she gets the answer she wants. She taught me that. But what answer does she want from me?

She spins around, as if trying to catch me doing something, and I hug the pillow tighter. "Why did you pick these particular people to put on your wall? What were your criteria?"

"Kids don't have *criteria*, they have impulses."

"Okay, then, which impulses made you choose these particular faces?"

I slide down on the bed and pull the pillow over my head. Suddenly I'm seeing pillow, feeling pillow, breathing pillow. My world is pillow.

She tugs it off me. "All right, you don't have to tell me. You can relax."

"I'm relaxed."

She takes a long, deep breath as if she's the one who needs relaxing. She used to do my breathing exercises with me in the living room. Now she mostly does her back exercises, rolling up on the floor and rocking back and forth. She looks kind of like a giant flipped-over snail.

"I haven't told anyone at the school about your tendencies, Devon. I wanted you to know that."

Mom has a nice way of putting things. When we moved to Amherst after my grandfather died, I developed a *ten-*

dency to wash my hands, a *tendency* to stay in my room, a *tendency* to eat foods in certain ways. If everybody had left me alone, there wouldn't have been any problem. But nobody ever leaves you alone. They always think they know what's best for you. I bet it's no different here in Belford.

She's staring down at me now, and I wonder how I could have such a pretty mother. Her face doesn't have one wrinkle on it. Doesn't she ever worry about herself?

"That's what you wanted, isn't it, Devon—a clean slate?"

What I want is to have no slate at all. Why is everyone always watching me? Aren't their own lives interesting enough?

"You can keep yourself under control. You've done it before for periods of time. If you get too anxious, you can go to the school nurse and tell her you don't feel well. She'll let you sit in her office for a while."

"I know the routine, Mom."

"I guess you do." She fluffs my pillow and puts it behind my head. "But it might be better if you develop a new routine rather than falling back on the old one."

What's the matter with the old routine? Is it a crime to wash your hands a lot and keep your books in alphabetical order? And what is so odd about doing things in fours? Lots of people have favorite numbers.

She picks up a picture of me with my old dog, Lucky, the two of us rolling in the snow outside our big Victorian home in greater Amherst. "It's funny—sometimes when I look at this I see two dogs playing with each other, and sometimes I see two children playing. I never see a dog and a boy."

I laugh at that, because here is my actual Mom thinking something totally strange.

*EnglishAlgebraBiologyLunchFreePeriodGymClassics
Done!*

When she leaves I straighten the edges of my paperbacks
so that they line up perfectly. I love that they're all 4¼ by 6¾
inches. That's all I buy now. Sure, they're different thick-
nesses, but that can't be helped. You can't tell every writer
in the world to write the same number of words. Besides,
it's height and width that matter, not thickness.

I put the lacquer box halfway between my old broken
stopwatch, which I used to time myself holding my breath
under water, and my Swingline stapler, which I've never
used because the staples come out crooked and I don't
have anything to staple, anyway. Then I take the chrome
Zippo lighter from my jeans pocket and put it back inside
the Chinese box. Mom won't look in there again for
months. I shouldn't have to hide it, since I don't smoke.
But she won't believe I just like holding my old Zippo and
flipping the top open. It makes a nice clinking sound,
open and close, open and close. I can do that for hours.

I leave the meditation stones as they are because
there's no way I can get them back exactly how they were.
Some things are like that. Some things that happen you
can make un-happen, but not everything. So I just rotate
the basket a little past ninety degrees to get the tag saying
"Made in Thailand" turned to the wall. After checking my
room for another minute, I'm ready to go downstairs to
eat dinner with the parents.

CHAPTER 2

I abominate dinner. That means I hate it. But I hate so many things that just for a change I like to abominate.

Sometimes at dinner my throat tightens up and I can't swallow, no matter how much water I pour in. But what's worse than eating with my particular parents are Dad's questions, which start with "How was your day?" My day always sucks, but I'm not allowed to use that word in front of them. So I say, "It could have been worse," even though usually I don't think it could have. I know there are kids in other countries who are forced to be slaves or prostitutes or soldiers. I see them on TV sometimes. If I were suddenly dropped into their world, things would definitely be worse. But in my world, my day always sucks.

My father's next question is even more irritating than his first: "What did you learn that was interesting today?" I never learn anything interesting during my day, at least that I feel like telling them. Besides, I don't like everybody eating and talking. It isn't polite. Sometimes the sloshy sound coming from my father's mouth makes me gag.

He wipes his mouth with his napkin, leaving a deep green smudge of chewed peas. "I heard something on the radio this afternoon that I thought was fascinating. If you took out the spaces between all the atoms of the nuclei in your body, you would end up half the size of a flea but still weigh the same."

Mom breaks open a roll so neatly that not even a crumb falls on her plate. I don't know how she does that. She looks at Dad. "I thought the human body was mostly water, not air."

He drops a gob of butter on his mashed potatoes. "Sure we're water, but I think it's inside the molecules of the water where all the space is. Of course, I'm no physicist, so I don't know if that's really true."

I break open my roll, and a few crumbs fall on the tablecloth. This is the kind of thing that's not supposed to bother me anymore, since my old shrink taught me ways to distract myself at dinner. The thing is, I don't want to be distracted. I just want to clean up the crumbs. So I sweep them up with my right hand and dump them on my bread plate.

I know they saw me. I have to distract them. "Wouldn't it be a biologist you aren't, Dad, not a physicist?"

He stares at me as if I'm making fun of him, but I'm really just wondering. What he actually is is a funeral director, which means he embalms people for a living. That makes me Son of the Embalmer. It sounds like some weird late, late movie on cable.

Dad breaks open his roll, and crumbs go flying. He leaves them on the table. "My point, Devon, is I'm not the kind of expert who would know if that's actually true about taking out the space in our bodies. I just heard it on the radio. Now, what did you learn today?"

I look away, pretending he isn't talking to me, and scoop out the center of my mashed potatoes with my spoon. Then I pour milk in, exactly to the rim.

Mom swallows fast. "I read something from Thoreau this morning." She often tries to bail me out when Dad asks me a direct question. She knows he makes me nervous. "It was on my daily quote calendar at work. He wrote, 'I wish I could worship the parings of my nails.' "

I spread my fingers out to take a look. My nails are nicely rounded, just a sliver of white extending to the edge of my fingers. I might be able to get into worshiping them.

Dad shakes his head. "I admire Thoreau as much as the next person, but sometimes he went off the deep end, don't you think?"

Now Mom shakes her head. "I appreciate his sentiment. Thoreau is trying to see the specialness of life in even the most insignificant parts of it."

The table is silent for a minute. That's the way I like it. Except I know the conversation is heading back at me.

"So, Devon, what do you have to tell us tonight?"

I have nothing. I never have anything. So I make things up. "Did you know Hitler had a cat?" They look at me with their this-is-even-weirder-than-usual expressions. "It was a stray he took in . . . in the bunker. He named her Muffin."

"Muffin?" Mom drinks some water from the huge mug Dad gave her for Christmas. It says "She Who Must Be Obeyed" around the middle.

"Muffin was the translation. In German it was something like *Das Muf-kin-izer.*"

Dad sips some water from his small glass. He doesn't like drinking water, but Mom says it's good for him and that coffee isn't. "I can't picture Hitler with a cat. A dog, maybe, like a schnauzer, but not a cat."

"He's kidding us, Frank." She opens her mouth in a perfect circle and inserts a piece of steak. "Aren't you, Devon?"

I shrug, leaving them wondering as usual, and stick my fork into the pile of peas on my plate. When I pull it out, there are five. I tilt the fork so that one falls off and then eat the rest. When I look up, they're watching. They probably saw me drop the one pea. I don't think it's so terrible, wanting to eat four peas instead of five. People do worse things every minute of the day, and who's staring at them?

I plunge my fork into the potatoes and shove a big clump into my mouth—they can't find anything strange about that! Then I lift my glass of water in two hands and gulp—one, two, three, four swallows.

Dad forks up a bunch of peas and eats them. "How did your first session go with Dr. Wasserman?"

I lick around the inside of my mouth until all the potatoes are gone. "Okay."

"What did you talk about?"

Mom puts down her mug of water. "You know you're not supposed to ask that, Frank. It's confidential."

"I *know* that the last doctor spent five months playing

Stratego and Battleship with Devon. I want to make sure this one's not doing the same thing."

Dad's wrong. I played Stratego and Connect Four with Dr. Castelli, not Battleship.

Mom liked my old shrink. He told her once that I was very well behaved and complimented her on raising me. I don't think he gave Dad any credit, and that's probably right since he never spent much time with me. Mom's the one who used to read to me every night. She played board games with me on the weekends and took me to museums. When we were out driving she would tell me about the divorces she was handling, and I always wondered if she'd divorce Dad someday. It's not that they have these terrible big fights or anything. It's just that they don't seem to fit together. Like, she's smarter than he is by a mile. And a lot more friendly. And nicer. I could go on and on.

Dad doesn't talk to me very much. I think he wanted a baseball-basketball-football-playing kid, since that's the type he was, growing up. After I got to be about eight, he stopped asking if I wanted to go out in the yard and have a catch. I never saw the point of catch. I never saw the point of sports, either. I told him that once, and he just shrugged and walked away.

Mom reaches for the pitcher of water and fills her mug. Dad says we should just hook up a hose to her. That's pretty funny—for him—but the thing is he says it about twice a day, so nobody laughs anymore.

"Therapy takes time, Frank. The doctor and Devon were establishing a relationship of trust with each other."

"Their *relationship* cost us two thousand dollars— that's outrageous."

Mom keeps eating her little mouthfuls. Dad taps his fingers on the table. It's the only nervous habit I've ever seen in him. They aren't looking at each other. It seems to me an odd way of arguing.

What I'd like is for Mom to throw a roll at him and Dad to toss a spoonful of potatoes at her, and then they'd splash each other with their water. That would be an interesting argument. I wouldn't even mind cleaning up the mess.

"How would you know therapy is outrageous? You've never tried it."

"Why would I try it? I don't need to pay somebody two thousand dollars and get nothing to show for it."

I agree with Dad—I have nothing to show for twenty sessions with Dr. Castelli except that I'm now an expert at Connect Four. I even went to the store looking for Connect Five, but they said the game doesn't exist. It's strange nobody has invented that yet. Maybe I'll do it.

I estimate that I agree with my father ten percent of the time and with my mother twenty-five percent. I think that's a pretty high total for a kid agreeing with his parents, but I don't know for sure.

Mom takes a bite of roll. "I'm just saying let's give it another try. A new therapist, a new school, a new town— let's give them all a try."

Dad nods. "Of course we're giving them a try. That's why we moved, isn't it?"

"Frank!"

What does he mean? I thought we came to Belford so Dad could expand his funeral business and Mom could find more people who want to get divorced. They said we moved closer to the city for greater opportunities, and I thought they meant their own. "You mean we moved because of me?"

Mom eats some of her potatoes. "We moved for everyone's sake, Devon."

I stick my fork into my peas and come up with three. They're watching me again. My hand is starting to sweat. They keep staring. I'll show them. I close my eyes and eat the three stupid peas.

CHAPTER 3

Later, in my room, I log onto the Net in order to have something to do besides think about myself. Dr. Castelli had five months and six days to figure out exactly why I am like I am and couldn't do it. That makes me wonder, could I be some new psychological phenomenon? I know I'm strange compared to normal kids, but could I be strange even within the whole world of strange people? That makes me feel really odd.

I call up google.com on the screen and search under "teenager," which I am, and "obsessive," which is the word Castelli used to describe how I kept my Connect Four chips in perfect piles of four before playing them. Two hundred and sixteen Web sites come up in .34 seconds. I like that google tells you how fast their search takes, but really, I wouldn't mind waiting a whole second. It's not like I have anything else to do in the two thirds of a second google saved me.

I click in and out of "personality disorder" and "depression" and "teen mental health" until I see a site saying, "What Is Generalized Anxiety?" Since Dr. Wasserman used that term at our first session today, I click on it and read: "Generalized anxiety is characterized by shakiness, muscle aches, soreness, restlessness, fatigue, and irritability. The sufferer is on edge and easily startled." That doesn't sound like me at all. I don't shake or ache that much. I'm not sore or irritable or easily startled. How could a shrink be so wrong?

I scroll down, clicking on every link, and come to "SocioPathways," by a kid named NOWAYNOTME. I like his name, so I keep reading:

"Controlling myself is not nearly as satisfying as controlling others."

I don't want to control others, but I do like controlling things, which is just as hard.

"I find humor in life by looking for people to laugh at."

I don't see the point of laughing at other people. Kids usually laugh at me, and they seem to have fun doing it, but I'm not into that.

"I like my personality flaws, because without them I'd have no personality at all."

NOWAYNOTME makes me wonder what my personality would be if I didn't have my "tendencies," as Mom puts it. If I weren't Devon the Anxious, Devon the Obsessive, Devon the Clean, what kind of Devon would I be? There wouldn't be much Devon left.

At least I'm not a sociopath, from what NOWAY says. Still, I click on "Chat" and register as Psychobabble, the user ID I always use. Then I enter the Sociopathic Chat Room.

"hi, just surfed in . . ."

JWGjr—"Welcome, Psychobabble, what brings you here?"

"i'm trying 2 figure out what i am."

JWGjr—"A noble effort. Perhaps figure out what you aren't and see what's left."

"i don't have that long i have 2 go 2 bed soon."

JWGjr—"Okay then try getting in touch with your inner sociopath."

"i'm not sure i have an inner 1 of those."

JWGjr—"Everybody does."

"how would i get in touch with mine?"

JWGjr—"Think terrible thoughts. Imagine the worst thing you would do to someone if you could and not get caught."

"is that all?"

JWGjr—"No, this is important—you can't feel guilty about your thoughts. Get rid of guilt and there you will find your inner sociopath."

"thnx JWGjr out."

I log off feeling pretty good about the Sociopathic Chat Room. It's not often on the Net you find someone as friendly and helpful as JWGjr on the first posting. I decide to follow his advice. I close my eyes and think of dismemberment—and not just arms and legs, either. I think of squeezing someone's eyes until they pop and sticking sharp objects down his throat. I try imagining doing these terrible things to people, but each time an actual face passes through my mind, I feel guilty and ashamed. I wouldn't make a very good sociopath, and I'm glad. The world already has too many of them.

CHAPTER 4

I get nervous on first days—first anythings, in fact. There's always too much to figure out. Beginning school in January means I'm the only new kid. Everybody will be watching me.

Right now I'm watching them. I'm leaning on one of the huge columns outside of The Baker Academy pretending to be interested in the jagged outline of downtown Boston in the distance. I'm actually counting the kids going in the school. I don't know why I am—it's just something for my mind to do. But then as I count five and six and seven, it seems right that I should be the eighth kid going in, a multiple of four. Before I can reach the door a girl comes running up the steps and butts in front of me. So I go back to leaning and counting . . . nine, ten, eleven. My chance comes up again, but this time two kids get there first.

This is getting weird. It's never mattered before what number I was going in a door. I should just go in. I can do it. All the other kids are. But it seems to me that I can use all the luck in the world today, and that means using my lucky number. The 7:55 bell rings. Fourteen kids have gone in since I've started counting. I need one more. A tall girl comes up the steps—the tallest girl I've ever seen. I pretend I'm fixing something in my backpack so she won't think I'm staring, and she goes by me and inside. I follow her to the door. I pull out the tail of my T-shirt and stick my hand inside it to grab the handle. I yank open the door like that and then feel somebody behind me. I turn and see an older kid looking at my hand in my shirt holding the handle. He must think I'm crazy.

"I have a cut on my finger and didn't want to get blood all over the handle."

"Whatever." He shrugs and squeezes past me into the school. There's no one else coming. I have to go in, the seventeenth kid. This is not a good start.

In the rear of tenth grade English, I'm sitting straight, my elbows on my desk and my hands folded, which is my best position for blocking out distracting thoughts. The teacher, Ms. Hite, is talking so fast about "The Raven" that there isn't time for me to think about anything else. I like that. Suddenly she slaps shut her poetry book. "All right, class, in the remaining thirty minutes I want you to write an essay: Why does the raven repeat, 'Nevermore'? Any questions?"

I have a question—am I supposed to do this assignment? She doesn't see my hand. I know this poem because it was my grandfather's favorite, and I read it to him probably fifty times. I could fake a pretty good answer. Still, I don't want to write the paper if I'm not supposed to.

"You may begin."

So I begin. I open the maroon and white The Baker Academy notebook that Mom bought for me and write, "Nevermore—What the Raven Means."

I scan the poem in my textbook. ". . . its answer little meaning—little relevancy bore." That means the man in the poem doesn't even understand the raven, so how are we supposed to? I start writing:

> In the poem "The Raven," by the famous writer Edgar Allan Poe, the main character asks a question of the raven six times, and six times the bird says, "Nevermore."
>
> The man wants to know if he'll be reunited with Lenore in Heaven—"Nevermore."
>
> He wants to forget Lenore because thinking about her is driving him mad—"Nevermore."
>
> He tells the raven to leave ("Take thy beak from out my heart, and take thy form from off my door!")—"Nevermore."
>
> I think the raven is like the part of a person's mind that keeps saying everything's going to be bad. No matter what the man asks, the raven says no. He will always suffer thinking of Lenore. He will never get her out of his mind.
>
> The raven says "nevermore" because it is a word that means something won't ever happen, and it's hopeless to hope. Also, "nevermore" rhymes with Lenore, which is important. If the raven had said "nope" instead of "nevermore," nobody would think this poem was very good.

"Time's up." Ms. Hite sweeps around the room collecting the papers. I hand her mine. She looks surprised. "Oh, Devon, you didn't have to do this assignment." Then she gives me back my paper and laughs like I've done something funny.

EnglishAlgebraBiologyLunch!

I've made it through my first morning of classes at The Baker Academy. It's one of the best private schools around Boston—that's what Dad says. Nobody calls it Baker or even Baker Academy. It's always The Baker Academy, or just The Academy, as if there aren't any others.

I felt panicky only twice so far today after coming in the front door. Once was in advanced biology, where there are these giant posters of different life forms hanging on the walls. The amphibians poster is crooked. The right corner is an inch higher than the left, maybe more. Crooked things didn't used to bother me that much, but I couldn't stop staring at that poster this morning. I tried looking at primates and reptiles, which were straight, but my eyes kept going back to amphibians. Finally I leaned down a little and put my hand over my eyes. After a minute the teacher, Mr. Torricelli, asked me if I was sleeping. I said no, and to prove it I repeated everything he had just said—that humans have only fifty percent more genes than a roundworm, twice as many as a fruit fly, and five times as many as slime mold. I can remember stuff like that, no problem. He didn't seem impressed. He still told me to keep my head up, so I had to stare at the crooked poster for the whole hour.

Then after advanced biology I was walking down the hall past the gym, and there's a metal railing around the bleachers. I touched the top of the first support post and the second, and the third. But there were a couple of kids leaning near the fourth post. I waited for a minute, figuring they'd soon move away to their class. But they didn't. They were laughing and talking. One of them glanced toward me, and I knelt down to retie the laces of my sneakers. When they were all looking the other way I sneaked along the railing and reached under the kid's arm to touch the support.

He whipped around on me. "What are you touching me for?"

I said it was an accident. I said I was sorry. Then the bell rang, and we all took off running to our classes.

He probably thinks I'm a real wacko. He might tell the whole school. But at least I touched the fourth support.

Now for lunch. I walk down the long back corridor, hunting for an out-of-the-way place to eat. I pass the cafeteria, and it's as loud and messy as I expected. Kids are talking and eating and laughing and playing cards—it's a lot like my old cafeteria, except for the huge flags of the world hanging from the ceiling. And the black kids and white kids are eating together, which is strange. How did the school get them to do that?

At the end of the hallway I come to a door. There's no sign saying "Emergency Exit Only," so I swing my hip against the release bar. The door opens on to a small parking lot full of cars. It's cold, but I've eaten in colder places back at Amherst Regional. I zip up my winter jacket and sit on the top stone step. When I open my lunch bag I see that Mom gave me exactly what I asked for—four small carrots, one peanut butter sandwich cut in squares, one small bottle of Evian water, four vanilla wafers and four M&Ms, all different colors. She wants me to have a good day, too. I eat the wafers first, then the M&Ms—yellow, red, green, brown. Sometimes I eat them brown, green, red, and yellow. Colors don't really make any difference to me.

"Hi."

I look up and there's a thin black girl in a ski jacket coming through the door carrying a frozen ice cream cone. "Hi."

She peels the wrapping from her cone. "I saw you in English—you're new, right?"

"Yeah, I'm new."

"Don't like the cafeteria?"

I shake my head. "I never eat in cafeterias."

"Me either. How come you don't?"

School cafeterias are disgusting, that's why. If you inspected the tables under a magnifying glass you'd see bacteria that look like buffaloes. The orange plastic trays have probably been thrown up on by hundreds of kids. Think of how many mouths the forks have been stuck in. Think of all the lips that have sucked on the spoons and the tongues that have licked the knives.

I can't really tell the girl any of this, because she'd call me a wimp. Before I can think of a fake reason, she starts talking again.

"Kids don't hassle you much in this school, if that's what you're worried about. They leave you alone."

"It's not that, really. I just like eating by myself at lunch."

She picks up her backpack. "That's cool. You can have this place."

"No, I didn't mean you."

She sits next to me on the steps. Her green sneaker touches my green one. Her thin leg touches my thin leg. I've never been this close to a black girl before, and I think she has the most beautiful skin I've ever seen. It's like dark syrup. I can't stop looking at her thick pink tongue, which turns white with each swipe of the ice cream.

She tilts her cone my way. "Want some?"

"No, thanks." I eat a square of my peanut butter sandwich. I should offer her one, but what if she accepts? What if she takes a little bite and then hands it back to me? She'll think I'm racist if I don't eat it. I'll offer something she can't give back. "You want my carrots?" I pull the plastic bag of them from my lunch bag.

She shakes her head. "I never eat anything for lunch except a vanilla cone."

"*Never*? Every single day you eat a vanilla ice cream cone?"

"Yeah, every school day. Except once last year they only had chocolate, and I was like really weirded out for the whole day. You know what I mean?"

I know exactly what she means.

She licks a drip of ice cream from the cone. "So, what are you into?"

Lacrosse, wrestling, swimming, drama, the Latin club—I could say anything because how would she know I won't do any of them? "Nothing much. I just hang out."

"No sports or clubs or anything?"

I always thought I might go out for a sport where people don't sweat, but I don't think there is one. I don't mind sweating myself, but other people? I'm not into that. Most activities I can think of mean getting so close to someone that you're breathing in the air they're breathing out. That's pretty disgusting. Maybe if Dr. W. works a miracle I could go out for something, but I'm not ready yet.

"I'd be in an animals club, if there was one."

"You mean, like rabbits and frogs?"

"Actually, I'm into predation."

"Predation?"

"You know, wolves, big cats. The world's divided between predators and prey. I like the predators."

She turns over the cone and sucks through the hole in the bottom. The door opens again and a freshman-size kid looks out, sees us, and ducks back in. The door rattles closed.

"You single?"

Me, married? Is she crazy?

She doesn't give me time to answer again. "I've been single since Thanksgiving. It's cool. No hassles, you know? Except now guys try to bust a move on me all the time 'cause they know I dumped Alonzo. He was my main man for three months. He was, like, all hands, you know? I got tired of that."

So at this school *single* means not going steady. There could be hundreds of other words they use differently here. How am I supposed to learn them all?

"I'm single, too. I've always been single."

"I figured."

That sounds like an insult, but I'm not sure, because she isn't laughing at me. Usually I don't care what other kids think, but this girl makes me wonder. "You think I'm hopeless with girls?"

"Not hopeless, just kind of clueless." She pulls off the end of the wrapper and stuffs the rest of the cone in her mouth. Then she hoists her backpack to her shoulder and waves goodbye.

She's leaving too soon. I don't know anything about her. "Hey, how come *you* don't eat in the cafeteria?"

She screws up her face and taps her nose. "Can't stand the smell."

I've never seen a teacher like him. He glides up and down the rows like some large black bird, his robe swirling around him. He pauses and looks at the ceiling, or the blank blackboard, or the empty walls, as if seeing something there we can't. He speaks almost in a whisper, and I'm leaning forward like all the other kids to hear.

"The Greeks were the first intellectuals. They invented philosophy and exalted their philosophers to the height of kings in other lands."

I know about the Greeks, and Romans, too. Mom read Bulfinch's *Mythology* to me every night for months. She made me take Latin in middle school when almost every other kid was learning Spanish or French. I wonder what it would have been like to be born in Greece back then— would I have been a philosopher-king, a soldier, a peasant, a slave, or someone even worse off, like a woman?

The teacher stuffs his hands into the pockets of his

robe, and now he's all black, except for his little white face sticking out at the top. "And yet, the ancient Greeks were profoundly ignorant, in our modern sense. They knew nothing of the world beyond the hundreds of miles their ships sailed and their troops marched. They believed the earth was a circular flat disc divided by the Sea, what we now call the Mediterranean. Surrounding the earth was water, and each morning the sun rose from the waters in the east and each night dipped back into the waters in the west. In this ocean they imagined giants and monsters and enchantresses. Beyond the ocean they could imagine nothing."

How can anybody imagine nothing? If the Greeks could invent gods who disguised themselves as bulls and swans and turned people into spiders and flowers, then they certainly could have dreamed up something interesting for the world beyond the ocean. What kept them from exploring the far-off seas? Maybe they were just happy with the life they had.

The teacher walks to the huge windows at the side of the room and stares out for a minute. The students stare with him. Nobody throws a pencil or makes some stupid noise. I've never been in a class this quiet.

"The Greeks had their gods—Zeus, the most powerful; Pallas Athena, the goddess of wisdom; Apollo, the god of music and prophecy; Aphrodite, the goddess of love and beauty; Ares, the god of war. Citizens of Hellas would appeal to one or another of them depending on what favor they needed. But Greek philosophers such as Socrates, Plato, and Aristotle spent very little time considering the nature of their gods. The Egyptians before them focused on the spirit world and the afterlife. But the Greeks dedicated themselves to the matters of this world, the matters of man—truth, beauty, justice, citizenship, happiness."

The teacher picks up his Starbucks mug from his desk and drinks a little. I wonder if it's really coffee inside. "'Know thyself'—these words were inscribed at the Oracle of Delphi. Greeks journeyed there to ask about the future, and the first thing they saw was that saying, 'Know thyself.' Why would the great Oracle give that advice, above all else?"

No one raises a hand. The teacher looks annoyed. "Scholars?"

I'm used to answering at my old school. I always have something to say in class. Sometimes I don't even know what I'm going to say until the teacher calls on me. I start to raise my hand, then remember I'm new here. It's not good to speak up the first day.

"Mr. Brown, do you wish to contribute?"

Everyone turns on me, a blur of strange faces. I try to focus on the teacher in the black robe. "I think the Oracle at Delphi was just saying that people should look for answers about the world inside themselves, because how you look at the world changes it." That's not bad, and I got it out without my jaw locking up. Now the teacher will move on to somebody else. That's the way it works.

Except that he's still looking at me. "Would you say you know yourself, Mr. Brown?"

I think I do. I'm a pretty smart fifteen-year-old kid who

likes the world when it fits together exactly as he pictures it and who gets scared of the world when it doesn't. "Yes, I mean, I know who I am at this instant. But people change all the time, especially kids, because we're growing up. So today I'm different than yesterday, and tomorrow I'll be different than today."

"We all change, even old teachers like me. Perhaps tomorrow I'll come to class in a blue jumpsuit with white buck shoes."

The kids laugh at this weird image of him, and I do, too. It's nice to be able to laugh at a teacher.

"But I know myself, Mr. Brown, and I don't think I'll change that much by tomorrow." With that he turns back toward the front of the room, his long robe dragging behind him.

CHAPTER 5

"Well, Devon, I'm glad to see you again."

I wouldn't be glad to see me if I were Dr. Wasserman. And I'm definitely not glad to be standing in the middle of his crummy little office again. What is *glad*, anyway? It's a stupid word.

"Still don't feel like sitting?"

"No . . . I mean yes. I don't feel like sitting."

"What if I throw a blanket over the chair, would that make it okay?"

I shake my head. I'd still know what's under the blanket. The shrink opens his wallet. "You know, I'd feel more comfortable if you did sit down. All of my other patients do. So I'll tell you what—I'll give you twenty dollars if you'll sit in the chair." He points with his hand that holds the money to the shiny vinyl seat behind me.

"I really like standing."

He takes another twenty-dollar bill from his wallet. "How about forty?"

He's messing with my head, I can tell.

"Would you sit for sixty dollars?"

I don't like this at all. What kind of shrink would try to force a kid to do something he really, really doesn't want to do?

"Just so we're clear here, Devon, at some point I'm going to put the money back in my wallet and the offer will be gone. You shouldn't think you can just hold out for more."

I bet Dr. W. will go higher. It would be too weird to stop at sixty dollars. He takes out two more twenty-dollar bills. "How about one hundred? It's yours just for sitting down on the chair, or the sofa—either one, your choice."

When I look at the vinyl chair with the little yellow stuffing sticking out of the rip, I see all the fat old people squatting down in it, all of the squirmy little kids' asses, all of the farting and sweating that has happened on that cushion.

I hear a ripping sound and turn—Dr. W. is tearing a check from his checkbook. "Why don't you just fill in an amount?" His chubby index finger points to the space next to the dollar sign. "Write whatever amount of money I'd have to give you to sit in that chair, and we'll see if I can afford it."

I take the check by the left edge. It's beautiful. Sailboats are gliding in a light blue sea so clear I can imagine diving in and never coming up again.

"Here's a pen."

He was holding it at the top, so I take it by the bottom,

very close to the tip. I know this is just some kind of shrink's game, but I have to admit, it's a pretty good one because I can't figure out how to win at it. If I write down $1,000 and Dr. W. actually gives me the money, then I'd have to sit in the vinyl chair or sofa. If I won't sit, then I don't get the money. Either way, I lose something.

I put the check up against the wall and write 1,000, which is a nice round number. I shake the pen to get the ink flowing again, then add a 0, then another one, and another. I hand the check back to Dr. W.

"One million dollars. That's a bit more than I was expecting. Is that what it would take to get you to sit in that chair?"

"I'm not sure, maybe more."

"Well, I guess you might as well stand, then." Dr. W. puts away his money and his checkbook. So I've lost a hundred dollars. He opens a thin manila file folder. "I called your mother yesterday to get some perspective on what happened when you lived in Pennsylvania."

Pennsylvania—why does he have to bring that up? I was a little kid then.

What happened is that I couldn't stop snapping my fingers. I know that sounds stupid, but it's true. It started with my granddad, when he moved in with us because of his bad heart. One night he was feeling pretty weak, so I stayed up late in his room reading *The Fortunes of Captain Blood* to him. I had just started the chapter where Blood escapes hanging, and I knew my grandfather would love that part. But after a minute his eyes closed. I kept reading, thinking he was still listening, but he didn't smile or nod. So I made up a few crazy sentences, and he didn't say anything. He looker stiller than I'd ever seen him. That scared me, so I put my left hand on his chest. I started snapping the fingers of my other hand in time to the faint beating, and it seemed to me his heart was going awfully slow. After a while I pulled away and was going to go to bed. It was almost midnight. I was tired, too. But he didn't look like he was breathing. I went back to his bed and felt for his heart again. There wasn't any beat. I slipped my hand under his nightshirt. Nothing. Then I snapped the fingers on my right hand. One, two, three, four—I felt the beat. He had come alive again! I kept snapping my fingers, kept feeling his heart beating.

I don't know how long I did that, because I fell asleep in the chair next to his bed. Next morning I woke up early. No matter how much I shook him or snapped my fingers, he wouldn't open his eyes.

"Devon, I was asking about Pennsylvania. Could you explain the problem you had in school when you lived there?"

"I was snapping my fingers a lot, that's all, and it got on the teacher's nerves. Some of the kids didn't like it, either."

"If you knew you were bothering them, why did you continue to snap your fingers?"

"I don't know—I just did. It became a habit."

"How long did you have this habit?"

"A couple of months. Then we moved to Amherst and I stopped."

"But you started up other habits there, didn't you?"

Sure I did—washing my hands, straightening things,

staying in my room. All kinds of things started then. I close my eyes and try to stand perfectly straight, but after a few seconds I feel myself drifting forward.

"Devon?"

"I don't want to talk anymore about that stuff, okay? That was before."

"Before what?"

"Before now."

"All right, then let's talk about now, and here. Your mother says you eat the same lunch every day—four carrots, four wafers, four . . ."

"Lots of kids eat the same thing every day. I met this girl the first day at my new school, she eats a vanilla ice cream cone every single lunch, and she's been doing that for years. I've only been eating what I eat since September."

He nods like he understands, but I don't think he does. "What would happen if your mother gave you three carrots instead of four?"

I'd throw them away, that's what. "I'd eat them. It's no big deal."

"I'm not so sure. I think you're afraid something bad will happen if you don't have four carrots, four wafers, and four different colored M&Ms for lunch."

What makes him so smart about me? This is only my second time with him. Dr. Castelli couldn't figure me out after twenty sessions. "Are you sure something bad *won't* happen?"

"No one can guarantee that, Devon. But does it make sense to you that eating four carrots will stop something bad from happening to you or someone else?"

I know it doesn't make sense when you think about it for very long. I'm not stupid. Still, when I'm getting ready to eat those carrots or wafers or M&Ms, it seems very important to have exactly four of them, as if the universe depends on it. If you do one little thing wrong, the whole world could go out of whack—tilt off its axis, for instance, or drop out of the sky. Maybe it wouldn't happen, but nobody can prove to me that it *couldn't*. Why take the chance?

The shrink swivels in his chair, and it makes a squeaking noise. Hasn't he ever heard of WD-40?

"I'd like you to think about my question before next session, Devon."

"What question?"

"If it makes sense that eating four carrots—four everything—at lunch will stop something bad from happening."

"Okay, I'll think about it."

"By the way, do you know if you have ever had a severe case of strep throat?"

"No."

" 'No' you don't know, or 'no' you haven't had strep?"

"No I don't know—that's what you asked."

"Yes, well, ask your parents for me, will you?"

"I broke my arm once when I was ten, does that make any difference?"

"No, not for the purpose of understanding the source of your behaviors. Now, tell me a little about your parents."

I don't know where to start except at what they look like. "Mom's about five-eight—I got taller than her last summer. She has reddish hair like me and brown eyes like me and she's kind of skinny like me and she has small ears like me. They're not so wicked small that you laugh at them or anything—if you're the kind of person who laughs at people, I mean. Just regular small."

"You think your ears are too small?"

I reach up to trace the outline of my ear. They feel small to me. "They're not super small. Like, I can hear fine. I think I have perfect pitch."

"That's nice, but do you stare at your ears a lot?"

"How would I do that?"

"In the mirror."

"Oh yeah, well, maybe sometimes I do. Is that crazy?"

"It's not uncommon for adolescents to fixate on a particular part of their body because it seems odd or disgusting to them. But if they spend more than an hour a day focusing on some part, it could be a problem called body dysmorphic disorder."

That doesn't sound like something I want to have. "I look at my ears in the morning for ten minutes, tops. So I don't have what you said."

"Is there any other part of your body that seems small or odd to you?"

What's he mean by that? I look out the window, and the bright sun tickles my nose. I just get my arm in front of my face to block my sneeze. Dust floats up in the shaft of light coming in the window. "Sorry. I can't stop myself sometimes."

"That's okay. There's no law against sneezing in here."

A law—that's a great idea. No Sneezing Allowed! Wear Gloves When Touching Doorknobs! Don't Talk into Somebody Else's Face! I can imagine hundreds of laws. They'd be printed up and mailed to every person so nobody could say they didn't know. Kids would be taught the laws in kindergarten, then reminded of them each grade after that. And every one of the laws would have a ! after it!

"Devon? I asked if there is any other part of your body that seems too small to you, or odd in some way."

It's not a question a shrink should ask a kid, that's what I think. "No, everything's perfect. I wouldn't change a thing."

He looks as if he doesn't believe me, and why should he? I don't believe myself.

CHAPTER 6

It's Saturday. I can't tell exactly what time on Saturday, because I'm lying in bed facing my wall instead of my nightstand, and I don't feel like rolling over to look at the alarm clock. I guess it's around noon, because the sun is shining almost straight down through the skylight.

I know I should get up, but for what? I've got nowhere to go. The snow's half a foot deep outside. I'd go sledding if I had a hill out back. I know that sounds dopey—fifteen years old and he wants to go sledding. I can't help it. Maybe I suffer from arrested development. I suffer from everything else, why not that? If I had a little brother I could take him sledding and pretend I was being a great older brother, but I'd be having as much fun as him.

I love snow. At least, I love it when it's snowing and even the air is white. I love it the first day after a snow, too, when the trees and roads and ground are white. Snow covers the whole world, and for a few hours you only need to think about one thing. Snow.

"Lunch is ready, Dev. Come on down now, please."

I roll over and raise my hand over my head to block out the sunlight. I can see one thick blue vein bulging up at the bend of my arm. Or is it an artery? Arteries take blood away from the heart, veins bring it back, so I guess this is a vein. I don't know where I learned that. It was probably one of Dad's dinner lectures.

I wonder why there's no word for this part of the arm. Why didn't Mr. Elbow or whoever the person was who picked *elbow* for the outside of the bend of the arm name the inside at the same time?

The vein dives deep under the skin of my forearm and then comes up again at my wrist alongside another vein heading from my hand. If there were a hundred hands sticking up into the air like this, could I pick this one as mine? I don't think so. There aren't any rings or scars. The fingers aren't especially fat or thin. They're just fingers. On a hand.

"Devon, do you hear me? You've been in that bed for fourteen hours."

The hand seems to hang in the air as if suspended from invisible string. The fingers are curling down slightly now, the blood draining from them, I guess, heading back to my heart.

"I'm not calling you again."

Oh yes, she will. She'll badger me and threaten me until I go down and eat. She never leaves me alone when she thinks it's for my own good.

I lift my head off my pillow, and the hand falls to the bed.

■ ■ ■ ■

She's made ham omelets. I poke at the gooey mess and scrape out each little piece of meat.

"What are you doing?"

"I'm vegetarian—remember, Mom?"

"I don't care. You need more protein." She pushes the ham back into my eggs with her fork. "That could be the problem."

She's always coming up with new explanations, and this one, the nutritional reason, is her latest. She thinks I'm not eating enough protein or drinking enough water or getting enough iron. Any one of those things could throw my brain chemistry off track and affect my thinking.

She said I should use my mind to control my impulses, but I don't see how that would work. If I'm not thinking right to begin with, how is thinking going to help me straighten myself out? It's like using a warped old yardstick to measure itself to see if it's exactly a yard long. Okay, maybe it isn't exactly like that, but I'm still sure it's useless to try to think myself into thinking normally.

She comes up behind me, a big shadow over my plate. "You're not eating, Devon."

I put a big forkful of the omelet into my mouth and stuff in a wad of sourdough bread just to please her.

CHAPTER 7

I never took biology in Amherst, so I don't know why they stuck me in *advanced* biology at The Baker. Mom says, "Your reach should exceed your grasp." Or maybe it's "Your grasp should exceed your reach" that she always says. I can't remember. What she means is, a person should do something that's challenging, not take the easy path. She's probably the one who signed me up for advanced biology.

So I take my seat again in the rear, just in front of jars full of dead things, such as frogs and mice and one small, coiled cat that looks like it has been shaved with a razor and then boiled. It's terrible seeing animals like that. I'd rather see dead people in jars than animals.

I've seen plenty of actual dead people. I'm the only kid I know who has a father who embalms people for a living. He said I could watch him prepare a body anytime, that I'd learn a lot about human anatomy. I've helped out directing cars and carrying flowers at funerals, but I won't go near the embalming room. Dad's hoping I'll take over the business from him some day. I told him that the only way I'd become an embalmer was over my dead body. He just laughed like I was making a joke.

Anyway, my teacher, Mr. Torricelli, starts talking with a big grin on his face, like some guy on TV trying to sell you a car. I watch his mouth so that I won't have to look at the crooked amphibians poster on the wall behind him.

"Today, class, we're moving on to primates." He bends down behind his display table at the front of the room and comes back up holding a life-size stuffed chimpanzee. Some kids whistle. A few make gagging sounds.

I can't believe what I'm seeing. A real dead chimp! He has this frozen, surprised look on his face that makes me wonder what he was doing when he died. Maybe he was heading up into the trees to be with his wife-chimp or kid-chimp. Or maybe he was a laboratory animal that they stuck with syringes full of HIV to see if he'd get AIDS.

Mr. Torricelli holds up the chimp in one hand, like a huge puppet. "This is Charley . . ."

I cover my ears, but I can't block out the booming voice of my advanced biology teacher. "Common yeast has a 30 percent overlap of genes with humans. Worms— 40 percent. Cows—90 percent. Another human being has 99.9 percent of the same genes as you, and a brother or sister, 99.95 percent. You and Charley here share 98.6 percent of your DNA. That means there is only a 1.4 percent difference, genetically speaking, between him and you."

I don't care about his genes. I want to know how this creature ended up here. What was he thinking when he was caught? What was he going to do next?

Mr. Torricelli leans back on his desktop, with Charley on his lap. "Because chimps are so similar to us in biological terms, they make very good subjects in experiments when scientists can't use humans."

Why not use humans, if that's who's going to benefit? I can think of plenty of people to experiment on.

Mr. Torricelli lifts Charley next to him on the desk and pats him on the back. "We sent a chimp into space before humans, and we test drugs on chimps. They are very intelligent creatures."

"This is terrible."

"Mr. Brown, did you say something?"

I guess I did, but I shake my head that I didn't. I meant only to think that it was terrible for him to be showing a dead chimp, but the words just popped out. Sometimes that happens to me.

"This chimp was seven years old when he died, and—"

"I hate this."

"Mr. Brown, were you addressing me?"

I shake my head again. "No, I wasn't addressing you. Idiot."

Idiot? Did I just call my teacher an idiot?

He comes to the head of the aisle, carrying the chimp in his two hands. "If you have something to share, Devon, say it loud enough for everyone to hear."

I stand up. The other kids are looking at me.

"I was just wondering how you can hold up a dead animal and act like it's all right to kill him for experiments."

"This is how we learn about things in science."

"Well, how would you like being stuffed and held up by a chimp teacher in a world run by chimps so that *they* could learn?"

"Mr. Brown, your question is out of line. Please go out into the hall."

Charley's staring at me. If I leave, he won't have anyone in the room who cares about him.

"You're new in this class and not familiar with the use of animals in our teaching. If the sight of this chimp upsets you, you can go outside for air."

I walk up the aisle, staring at the leathery fingers of this beautiful creature. Sure, I can leave, but what about him?

"Devon Brown—King of the Monkeys!"

I twist around to see who said that, but all the faces look the same to me, just stupid grins. "He's not a monkey. He's a chimpanzee."

I feel a grip on my arm. It's Mr. Torricelli's hand curling around my wrist. The sight of those pale, hairless fingers on me almost makes me sick. I grab the stuffed animal and run.

I don't get far. The hallways are empty, and I manage to duck past the physics and chemistry classrooms and then take the turn toward the front exit without being seen. But coming in the big glass doors are Coach Duffy, my gym teacher, and Felix the janitor, who always wears a jacket that says "Felix" on the back.

I try to act casual. "Hey, Coach."

"Hello . . . Devon, right? You're the new sophomore?"

"Yeah, I'm new all right."

"What do you have there?"

"This is a chimpanzee. Mr. Torricelli was telling us about how close they are to humans—it's like we're almost identical, you know?" I hold the chimp's face up to my own, side by side. "See the resemblance?"

"Could be your twin brother."

"Yeah, that's funny. Anyway, the thing is, we started noticing this smell in class, and it turns out Charley here's stinking up the place. Want a whiff?"

I hold out the stuffed animal, and the two men lean back a little. "That won't be necessary."

"Okay, well, I better be getting this guy outside for some fresh air, like Mr. Torricelli told me." I take a step toward the door.

Felix laughs as I pass him. "Nice job they gave you."

"You know how it is, Felix. They always stick it to the new kid."

Outside, the winter wind is whipping snow across the broad granite steps of the old school. The sky is cloudless, and I feel like I could become unglued from the earth and float up and out over the big houses and thin, curving streets and just keep going wherever the wind would take me. Charley and I could sail away together.

I've felt this way before. Like in Pennsylvania, when my grandfather died, I crawled onto the roof outside his room and waited for a storm to blow me away. I was only eight then. It wouldn't have taken much of a wind to carry me off somewhere I could forget about him. It's strange that to get over losing somebody you love you have to try not to think about him.

The air settles down a little, and Charley and I are still standing on the steps. It's pretty obvious we're going nowhere. I prop the chimp against the wall, face out, but I can't stand the big, sad eyes looking at me, so I turn him toward the brick.

Then I just wait for Mr. Torricelli or the headmaster or somebody to come find me.

CHAPTER 8

I guess The Baker Academy isn't one of those zero-tolerance places where you make one mistake and they toss you back to the public schools. I had to apologize to Mr. Torricelli for being rude to him, and they decided I wasn't ready for advanced biology, so they switched me to earth science. *EnglishAlgebraEarthScienceLunchFreePeriodGym ClassicsDone.*

The headmaster called Mom, of course, and suggested I see the school counselor once a week to discuss my "sensitivities regarding animals." She told him I was already seeing a therapist for other reasons, and she was sure Dr. Wasserman could handle that issue as well. I heard her side of the conversation on the phone. She was making a tuna casserole while she talked to him, with the phone stuck under her chin. That's how I knew this wasn't going to be a big deal with her. If a mom stops doing what she's doing when the school calls, then you know you're in trouble.

I'm not sure how I know this. There are just some things that sound so true that you know they must be. I certainly don't have much experience with trouble, at least the kind that gets adults really angry at you. My trouble is always the "we know it's tough on you" type, like when I flipped out in Amherst because a kid ate one of my M&Ms, or when I'm late for class because I'm in the boys' room washing my hands.

That doesn't happen much anymore—washing my hands in the bathroom, I mean. Mom came up with a solution. It's a little bottle of antibacterial sanitizer that I can carry around in my pocket. I just squirt a drop on my hands under my desk and rub it in. I don't even need water.

I used up the whole bottle in one day. Mom couldn't believe it. She doesn't remember what school's like. All day you have to sit in desks that other kids were sweating and sneezing in just a few minutes before. I try not to use the bathroom, but sometimes I have to, and then there are door handles and door latches and levers and spigots to deal with. It's pretty hard not to touch them, so I squeeze a few drops of the antigerm stuff on my hands. The directions on the bottle say that one drop kills 99.9 percent of all common bacteria. So I use four drops each time. I figure they should wipe out that last one tenth of a percent.

Mom said she'd only buy me two bottles a week, so I've been trying to make it go a little further lately. I open doors with my shirttail, I turn on spigots with a paper towel, and some days in the winter I wear handball gloves. They're cool black leather, and they make me look kind of tough, which is pretty ironic since I wear them because I'm so wimpy about germs.

"Free" period at school is supposed to mean that you can do whatever you want during it, right? Or even do nothing at all. At Baker it means you have to go to the library to do homework or research four days a week. The other day you must sign up for either art or music.

Music would seem the logical choice, since I have perfect pitch, as I said. I can tell what any note is just by hearing it, and whether it's sharp or flat. Mom says it's a gift that only one of every ten people has, and I shouldn't waste it.

Well, some gifts aren't worth the trouble of having them. It's like if your parents give you a fourteen-fret dreadnought Martin guitar for your sixteenth birthday. They're not buying it so you can sit at home in your room strumming chords to yourself. They expect you to be in class shows and play a song or two when relatives visit at holidays. So with my gift of perfect pitch, my parents expect me to join the chorus and be in school musicals. Imagine me standing in front of people, singing! All that breathing on the back of my neck—I'd probably faint and fall off the stage and crack my skull.

That's why I chose art for my Friday class and I'm sitting in Mrs. Cohen's class after lunch, pinning a fresh sheet of white paper to my drawing table. Art you can do by yourself, and the worst that can happen is that the teacher tapes your painting on the wall for people to see when you aren't there. I'll save my perfect pitch for singing in the shower at home.

The assignment today is to draw a structure, such as a house. That takes some planning. I open my metal tray of paints and moisten each little tub of color with a drop of water from my brush. I figure I'll do my old house in Amherst, which had six-foot windows in the front and a porch that went all the way around to the backyard. With my ruler and pencil I mark out where the horizon would be, about a quarter of the way up from the bottom. Then I block out my house on the right side of the paper, leaving room on the left for trees or cars or whatever I want. You never put your main object in the middle of your picture. You create tension by putting it to one side or the other, which I learned in art at Amherst. For some reason people like tension in pictures but hate it in their actual lives.

After fifteen minutes I've got my house outlined. Mrs. Cohen walks by me, stops for the smallest fraction of a second, and moves on to this kid with purple hair two desks up on my right. He has already painted a huge house right in the center of his paper. Now he's dipping his brush into a blob of green and yellow on his mixing board, and then he swipes it across the bottom, under the house.

Mrs. Cohen looks over his shoulder. "Grass isn't usually that bright. Try more green."

The kid doesn't even look up at her. "Crabgrass is bright."

"Houses aren't usually surrounded by crabgrass, Ren."

At least, I think she said Ren. It could have been Den or Len or Pen for all I know.

Mrs. Cohen walks on to the next student and tells her that her sunflowers, if that's what they are supposed to be, look more like black-eyed Susans.

The boy with the crabgrass glances around and gives

me an odd expression, like we're friends sharing a secret joke. Then he picks up his brush, jabs it into the yellow and paints his grass even brighter. He turns toward me again and I look away. When I look back he's brushing black paint all across his sky.

Mrs. Cohen comes down our aisle again after a minute and tells me that this is a one-hour exercise, so I better begin painting right away. Then she stops at the purple-haired kid's desk. "This is supposed to be a realistic portrayal of a building, and realism doesn't include those colors for grass or sky."

"I guess I misunderstood the assignment, Mrs. Cohen." He says her name like Co-hen. Then the hand holding his paintbrush reaches around the back of her and swipes her pant leg, just below her smock.

She jumps out of the way, twists around, and sees the mark on her white pants. "What did you do?"

It seems pretty obvious what he did—marked up the teacher.

"Oh, I'm sorry, Mrs. Co-hen. It was an accident. I was listening to the interesting stuff you were saying about realism, and I forgot about the brush in my hand. I guess I kind of touched you with it."

He's such a good liar, I almost believe him. She looks around and sees me watching. I could turn him in, but that's not the first thing you should do in a new school if you want the other kids to trust you.

He winks at me. "You better wash that out right away, don't you think, Mrs. Co-hen?"

She rushes toward the supply room, where there's a sink and soap. For the rest of class I can hear water running.

When the bell rings, I hoist my backpack to my shoulder and wait to let everyone else leave first. I have Physical Torture next, and if I get there after the bell, Coach Duffy might send me off for a late slip. By the time I get that from the headmaster's office the period will be half over, and there'd be no use changing into gym clothes, right? I could just sit in the bleachers, reading, and Coach would probably forget about me. I don't like wearing gym shorts. My legs look like they belong on a chicken—skinny and hairless. Why do schools have the right to make you show your body parts to people?

The art classroom is empty now, so I head through the door. There's Purple Hair waiting for me.

"You saw me, didn't you?"

He's wearing a brown leather jacket with some kind of writing on the arms. He's as skinny as me and shorter, so I'm not afraid of him.

"Yeah, sort of. I mean, I saw your brush touch her leg, but it could have been an accident, like you said."

I start walking down the hall, and he does, too.

"It wasn't an accident."

"Oh."

"I can't stand the way she's always telling everybody what to do. She's like a Nazi art teacher or something."

This doesn't sound right to me. "I think she's Jewish. You can't be Jewish and a Nazi."

"Sure, you can. Being a Nazi is like a state of mind. Anybody can be one."

We reach the door to the locker room, and the kid stops there with me. "You got gym now?"

I nod.

"I got English with Hite. She's another Nazi."

I nod again, although actually, Ms. Hite seems pretty cool to me. She drives an old blue Beetle, not one of those phony-looking new ones.

The kid punches me in the arm. "Maybe I'll see you after school, like at the buses or something."

"I don't take the bus. I walk."

"Me too, so we could walk together."

"Yeah, maybe." That seems the safest thing to say to a kid like this.

CHAPTER 9

It gets kind of tiring standing for a whole hour in the middle of Dr. Wasserman's office, so today I think I'll lean against the wall. I squeeze myself between the vinyl chair and the floor lamp to the only free wall space in the room and wait for him to begin.

It takes him eighty-three seconds to look up from his papers, which I know because that's how many beats of my heart I felt, and it beats exactly sixty times per minute.

"You want to stand there today, Devon?"

Want is a pretty tricky word, if you think about it. It should mean that you really feel like doing something. I don't really feel like leaning against this wall. I'm only leaning here because it's better than standing in the middle of the room. I only *want* leaning because I don't *want* standing today.

"I thought I'd try leaning."

"Okay. But the lamp is shining right in your face. Why don't you turn it off?"

I reach down and pull the metal string. The light goes out, and I feel cooler right away. But now I can see that the lamp is tilted a little. I nudge the shade straight, but it's still not right. I lean over and look under the shade and see that the socket isn't screwed in tight to the base. With a few twists, I fix it.

"Thank you, Devon. I see you're good at mechanical things."

"Screwing in a socket isn't really very mechanical. It's actually kind of simple-minded, if you want to know the truth."

He looks at me like I called *him* simple-minded, which I didn't. Although if you think screwing in a socket is being mechanical, maybe you are simple-minded.

"Well, Devon, I understand you had a situation come up at school."

I did? A situation? "What do you mean?"

"The confrontation with your teacher in advanced biology."

"Oh, yeah. I didn't know that was a situation. I thought it was just something that happened."

"Why don't you tell me about it?"

"Mr. Torricelli—he's the teacher—he was holding up this stuffed chimp and talking about how people experiment on them—I mean on real chimps, not the stuffed ones—because they're so close to humans in their genes. The real ones, I mean."

"Yes, I understand. And what he said made you angry?"

"What he was *doing* made me angry because I figure how would he like to be experimented on and then stuffed and held up for a bunch of chimps to laugh at?"

"You really empathize with animals, don't you?"

"What's that mean?"

" 'Empathize'? It means you sympathize with their situation—you feel their pain."

"Then why don't you just say 'sympathize'?"

"The words are slightly different. 'Sympathize' means you feel sorry for someone. When you 'empathize' you almost feel what they're feeling, you identify with them. That's what you were doing with that chimp."

"I identify with all animals."

It's not just animals, though. It's things, too. Back in Amherst I started feeling sorry for this old wooden chair Mrs. Greeley left out in her backyard. She could have taken it into the cellar before the snow started. She could have sanded down the seat and glued up the arms and restained it. But she just left the chair out there to freeze and crack. In the spring I know she's going to say it's in terrible shape and throw it away. It was a great chair once, I bet. I never even sat in it, but I could see it from my bedroom window at night when I looked out at the stars.

Another *thing:* there was a toy shop in Amherst called The Olde Toy Shoppe. It had one of everything for sale displayed in its big front windows. When I walked by one day I saw that the little stuffed owl that always sat on a stack of miniature books had fallen off. It was sticking head-down in a mound of marbles. For days it stayed like that. Every afternoon on my way home from school I checked that window—the owl was still head down in the marbles, like it had been shot from a tree. Finally I went in and said I wanted to buy the owl in the window. The saleswoman pulled a box from under the counter with an owl in it. I said that I wanted the actual owl in the display window. She told me that one was old and dusty. I had to make up something fast, so I said that my little sister was in love with that particular owl and she wouldn't be happy with anything else. And it was her birthday. The woman climbed into the display window to get the owl for me, but she wasn't very happy about it. The thing cost me a couple of weeks' allowance, and it got lost when we moved here to Belford. That bothered me for a couple of days, but I got over it.

"Devon, would you tell me what you're thinking right now?"

Tell him about Mrs. Greeley's chair or the fallen owl? Nobody should be able to make you tell what you're thinking. It's probably in the Constitution somewhere— everybody has the right to his or her own thoughts!

"I wasn't thinking anything very interesting. I've forgotten already."

"Well, your empathy with animals doesn't give you the right to disrupt a class. I'm sure you know that."

I don't want to talk about this. I wasn't wrong, really. I just did something that *seems* wrong. There's a big difference. Besides, the amphibians poster hangs crooked in that class. That's enough to drive a kid crazy, if that kid is me.

"Devon, could you look at me?"

I don't want to do that either. He has drippy eyes. His face is oily, like the skin of a cooked turkey.

"I asked you to look at me, Devon."

"I know."

"Can you do that for me?"

Sure I *could* look at him. My head swivels like most heads.

"I don't think I'm asking that much."

"No, you're wrong. You're asking everything."

"Why do you say that?"

"Because if I do what you want now, then you'll just ask me to do something else and then something else and—"

"Okay, I understand your point."

"—then something else and then something else. And it would keep getting harder not to do things, because you'd expect me to do more and more."

"Don't you do what people expect of you now?"

Mostly I do. I get good grades like Mom wants, and I do my chores without complaining like Dad wants, and I don't listen to porno music or swear at them or stay out late or hang with kids who smoke or drink. I do every assignment for school on time, and I speak up in class. I'm mostly a good kid. The thing is, I don't think I can take one more person expecting me to act like they want me to.

CHAPTER 10

For two weeks and four days I've walked around The Baker Academy as I did at Amherst, wearing my jacket and carrying all my books. But then the headmaster spotted me in the halls and asked if I hadn't been issued a locker yet. I said I had but liked carrying everything with me. He said everyone at The Baker Academy used their locker, and I could tell by his voice that he'd think it strange if I didn't, too.

So here I am at my locker, number 379, at the end of the row of lockers between the science and humanities wings. My combination: 18-26-7. Two turns to the right. One turn to the left. Then back to the right. 18-26-7. *18-26-7.* I hang up my coat on the hook and arrange the books for my afternoon classes on the little shelf. I close the door and get ready to latch the Master's lock. *18-26-7.* I can remember that easily. Just to be safe I wrote the numbers down on the cover flap of my algebra workbook, which is the one I've decided I'll always carry with me. I shove the lock bar into the hole, and it snaps shut like it will never open again.

I have earth science next, and I head down the hall. 18-26-7. Is that my combination? I open the flap to my algebra book and see the numbers . . . 18-26-7. I take a few more steps. But what if I wrote down the wrong numbers? What if the numbers I'm remembering and the numbers I wrote down are both wrong? I should find that out now.

I head back to my locker, passing the kids heading toward their science classes. I dial in the numbers . . . 18-26-7, and the lock pops open. I thought it would.

The hall is emptying fast. I'm going to have to hurry to make earth science. I push the lock closed again and take off in a run. But did I really lock it this time? I was doing it fast. Maybe the bar didn't go all the way in the hole. The lock could be dangling open, and some kid could get in and mess with my stuff. I do a quick U-turn back to my locker and check. It's tight.

The bell goes off for the start of third period. I'm going to be late to earth science.

This is why I hate using lockers.

The girl with the vanilla ice cream cone is sitting on the steps outside the back door when I push through with my lunch. She has a thick book spread across her lap. She doesn't look up at me, but she moves over a little to give me space to sit down. Her name is Tanya, which I know from hearing her called on in English class.

I take out my lunch bag and unwrap my sandwich squares. I asked Mom to stack them for me, and she did, except they got a little squashed in my backpack. I eat one square in two bites and take out the next. Tanya glances over, then goes back to reading. I want to say something to her, I just don't know what. I've been wanting to say something to her every day in English, but she sits on the other side of the room. Also, Alonzo is in the same class, and I swear he stares at her the whole hour. I sure don't want to get between him and Tanya.

I eat my third peanut butter and jelly sandwich square, and then the fourth. When I finish I fold up the plastic bag and put it back. I can tell she's watching now, so I try not to act weird. I reach into the bag of carrots and take one out and eat it. Then the second, and third and fourth.

Then the M&Ms. First the brown, then the green, then the red one, then the yellow.

She lets out a little breath of air, and I don't know what it means. She stands up like she's going to leave. I don't want her to. I have to say something. "It's not as cold today as last time, you know?"

She stares down at me. "You're talking to me now?"

"Sure."

"You walk by me in English like I'm invisible, and now you want to talk when it's just us?"

"Yeah, it's—"

"I'm not good enough to talk to in front of people?"

"No, it's not like that. I'll talk to you anywhere—I really will. I didn't know you wanted me to."

"I don't like being disrespected. It's all about respect, you know."

"I wasn't disrespecting you. I'm probably the least disrespecting kid you know."

She hoists her backpack to her shoulder. "Then talk to me in class sometime." She goes past me and heads back into the school, licking her vanilla ice cream cone.

It's hard to imagine—a girl actually getting mad at me for not talking to her. That makes me feel good, although I guess I should feel bad.

I finish my lunch and head inside. There's still a half-hour till fifth period, when I figure I'll do my English journal writing assignment for tomorrow. Having to write about my day every day is almost as bad as having to talk about it each night at dinner. Then every Wednesday I go to the shrink's and talk about things again. My life really isn't interesting enough to get all of this attention.

As I pass the cafeteria I see the jocks sitting at the center table under the flags and the geeks playing speed chess in the corner and the preppy kids talking on their cell phones. Even if somebody hosed down the whole place with Lysol, exterminating every single germ, where would I sit? I'm not a jock or geek or preppy, so what am I?

I feel like nothing. That doesn't really bother me, because the thing I can't understand more than anything else I can't understand is why kids want to belong to a group. So they can paint their faces and yell "We're number one" at the basketball game? *We* who? Maybe the kids who play are number one, but how can anybody sitting in the bleachers claim that? And what kind of stupid geek would write "Geeks Run the World," like I saw on the bathroom wall?

I get to the library early for my free period, and nobody's around, not even the librarian. I guess they don't worry about books being stolen at this school. I don't feel like starting my writing assignment yet, so I grab a *Baker Banner* from the checkout counter and sit down at one of the study desks.

The top headline says, "Have You Thought About Suicide?" which seems like a pretty interesting question for a school paper to ask. The article says that each year in the United States five to ten thousand kids kill themselves.

When I turn the page I see a questionnaire: "What's Your SP (Suicide Potential)?"

Have you ever had thoughts of committing suicide? I check the Yes box. Sure, I've thought about it. Hasn't every kid?

Have you thought about how you would commit suicide? Yes. By lightning—I'd stand in a lake during a thunderstorm holding my mom's metal tennis racket. That should do it.

What would cause you to commit suicide? Life. I suppose I should be more specific, but I don't want to rule out any good reasons.

If you were going to commit suicide, would you tell your best friend beforehand? What best friend? If you're going to commit suicide, you probably don't have one.

Has a friend ever talked to you about suicide? What friends?

What do you think are the warning signs that someone is thinking of committing suicide? Depression, anxiety, anger, failure, misery. And crying a lot, but maybe not so much for boys.

Suicide Suicide Suicide Suicide Suicide Suicide—six

times in six sentences. When you look at the word awhile, it makes no sense . . . soo-a-side, SOO-a-side, soo-a-SIDE. Sounds like a pig call.

I feel better about myself after reading this article. After all, I have no intention of killing myself like thousands of other kids. Just because I'm anxious and obsessive sometimes doesn't mean I'm desperate. Besides, the things I do don't bother me half as much as they bother other people. For another thing, suicide is painful, and I'm not into pain. The last thing I want is to end up as a slab of meat on my dad's embalming table.

CHAPTER 11

I don't want to wake up. I want to sleep and dream about a world where I can cruise two feet above the ground and fly up to the roof if I want to or zip around a corner faster than anyone can catch me. All I'd have to do is think— *Zoom, Devon, Zoom*—and it would happen.

"Time to get up, Devon."

Where do dreams come from? From the mind some-where, but which part—the part that wishes certain things to happen or the part that wishes other things wouldn't? I asked Dr. Castelli this question and he said, "Dreams may be the brain's way of getting rid of the odd images and feelings that accumulate during the day so you can wake up refreshed in the morning." If that's so, how come I wake up feeling like a dog that's been run over in the middle of the night?

"Devon, you have to get up this instant."

Why do I have to? Why wouldn't some other instant do just as well? Parents control the house, the money, the car, the food—why do they have to control time, too?

"If you don't get up, I won't drive you to Harvard."

Mom always has a threat like this. She knows I want to go into Cambridge and see what Harvard's like. I'm probably not smart enough to get in there. She didn't even make it, and I'm pretty sure she's smarter than I am. Still, it's some place to go on a Saturday. I need a destination.

"All right, I warned you."

"I'm up." I jump out of bed just as she pushes in my bedroom door. My boxers are sticking straight out in front. "Mom!"

"Oh, sorry, Devon."

I grab the blanket off my bed to hold in front of me. "Sorry"? I've always thought that the most useless word in the English language, because it can never undo what's done.

Harvard's cool. The library looks like a monument you see in Washington. The information flier says that it has 3.2 million books. I probably couldn't even read all the *titles* before I die. I walked around Harvard Yard all morning and went in the science building and the chapel and even a classrooms building. I looked in one of the rooms, and the kids were all hunched over their desks writing every word the professor said. And this is Saturday.

But the most interesting thing about Harvard is Harvard Square, which is where I'm standing now. I've never seen so many weird people all in one place. I'm trying to look at them without their knowing, so I've picked up a magazine at the Out of Town News, which is on a cement island in the middle of the traffic. The kids hanging out next to the subway entrance aren't much older than me. They have spiked hair and nose rings and dog collars around their necks. They're wearing black leather pants and black jackets and black boots. At Amherst we had one or two goth kids, but here there are dozens. How do they get away with it? I mean, don't they have to go home for dinner?

Imagine me dressed like that—Devon the Destroyer! I could do whatever I wanted, and who would mess with me?

"You buying that?" I look up and see a very short man with a pencil bobbing between his teeth. He nods at the magazine in my hands. "This isn't a library, you know."

Crochet World—why am I holding that? "Ah, no, sorry, I guess I don't want this after all." I slip the magazine back into its clip on the awning.

Behind me I hear laughter and turn to see a girl with silver sparkles on her face, shaking a can of whipped cream. She walks up to a guy holding a sign saying "Jesus Saves" and sprays the whipped cream on his head. The religious guy doesn't move—doesn't even turn around to see what the girl's doing. He just stands there. I know about being picked on, and this is strange. Why isn't he running away or fighting back? Then it strikes me—this guy wants to be picked on. He wants everybody to see how bad the kids are. Maybe he even wants to be persecuted, like Jesus.

This is too crazy, even for me. I cross the street and head up Massachusetts Avenue, past the Harvard Coop Bookstore. When I see C'est Bon I get thirsty. I wasn't thirsty before, but looking through the window at the big, cold bottles of Coke inside suddenly makes my mouth feel dry. I think I'm very suggestible.

When you think about it, "C'est Bon" is a pretty strange name. I mean, in France do they have "This Is Good" convenience stores?

I head for the door. I don't even stop to count the people going in, and I don't know why that is. Sometimes it matters, sometimes it doesn't. New obsessions are like that with me—they take time to take hold everywhere.

A ragged old man jumps in front of me, which is pretty rude. I wait for him to go in, but he just holds the door open, so I slip in around him. I find a tennis-ball can of barbecue chips and a sixteen-ounce Coke, which Mom won't buy for me because of all the caffeine. I pay the girl at the counter, then head for the door. It opens in front of me, and there's the same ragged man holding the handle. This time he has his hand out.

"Can you spare two quarters for my friend here?" He pulls back his old coat, and there's the smallest orange cat I've ever seen.

I want to pet him, but I'm not sure I should. Who knows what this guy might do?

"Go ahead. He won't bite."

I stick my finger toward the little face, and a paw reaches for it. I don't feel any claws. "What's his name?"

The man shrugs. "I don't know if he has one. I found him in the cemetery up the road last night. If you want to name him, go ahead."

The kitten opens his mouth and licks my finger. His

tongue probably has millions of germs on it, but I don't care. I wouldn't let any person in the world lick my finger, but this is a kitten. "Sasha, why don't you call him Little Sasha."

"Little Sasha. I like that."

I move out of the way to let a couple go past me. The man doesn't open the door for them. I don't know what to do next. I don't normally talk to beggars. Dad says they use your money to buy liquor. This guy doesn't look like a drunk. And he has Little Sasha. I pet the kitten again and then reach into my pocket. I pull out a fistful of change and three dollar bills. I keep two dollars and fifty cents for myself. "I need this to get home on the train, but you can have the rest."

The man smiles, and I'm surprised to see very straight, white teeth. "I don't need that much. Sixty cents will buy a small container of milk."

I drop two quarters and a dime into his hand. I hope he didn't notice I was making sure not to touch him. His hand is kind of curled up, like my grandfather's.

"May I presume on your kindness again, young man?"

"I guess."

"Could you buy the milk for me? They don't let you bring animals inside."

"Okay, or I could hold Little Sasha and you could go in and get what you want." He doesn't say anything. Maybe he thinks I'll run away with the cat. "I wouldn't hurt him. You can trust me."

"Oh, I trust you. But see, they don't really want people like me coming into their store." He sticks his finger through a hole in his jacket to show what kind of people he means. "And I don't like to go where I'm not comfortable."

Think of that—not ever going where you don't feel comfortable. If that were the case, where would I ever go?

CHAPTER 12

His name turned out to be Ben—the kid in my art class who marked the teacher. He must be a real loser in this school, because why else would he be waiting for me again after class the next Friday afternoon?

"Hey."

"Hey."

That's all we say to each other as we walk down the hall toward the gym. Just past the trophy case he nudges me to the wall, then whispers, "I got some ish. You interested?"

I don't know if I am or not. "Ish?"

"Yeah, some tree . . . herbal . . . smoke—man, where did you come from, anyway?"

"Intercourse."

"You got that right."

"No, I mean the town where I grew up in Pennsylvania was called Intercourse. The Amish named it."

Ben's grinning. Every kid grins when I tell him where I was born. "So you went to Intercourse High?"

"Intercourse Elementary, yeah."

Kids are rushing past us, going both ways. Nobody seems to be looking over, which means he's not a totally weirdo kid. He reaches into his pocket and then opens his hand between us, so only I can see. In his palm is a long, thin cigarette that looks like he rolled it himself.

"I'm skipping next period. Why don't you come with me?"

Skip class and smoke marijuana—is he crazy? "No, I don't do that stuff."

"That's cool. You don't have to. But come with me anyway."

"I've got gym now. I shouldn't miss it again."

"You hate it, right?"

"Yeah."

"So why are you running off to do something you hate?"

He's got a point. I'd do anything to get out of changing into those stupid gym clothes and showing my scrawny legs. Still, what if I get caught with a kid doing drugs?

Ben grabs my arm and pulls me down the hall to a door marked "Janitor." He checks both ways, then opens the door and yanks me through.

It seems like I've fallen into one of those video games where you slide through a pipe into a different world. I follow him down some grated metal steps to a large open area. It's loud and strange, like descending into the boiler room of the *Titanic*.

Ben leads us around stacked-up chairs and beat-up old

lockers and a huge box marked "This End UP," with the arrow pointed down. We duck under a large white air duct and turn into a room the size of a bathtub. On the floor is a straw mat and a blue plastic dish filled with butts.

Ben pulls out the cigarette and licks the wrapper to seal a loose edge. "It's my secret place. I never brought anybody here before."

"What about the janitors? Don't they come down for stuff?"

"They're cool. You slip them a few bucks and give them a hit and they leave you alone."

I can't imagine Felix taking a hit of oregano, let alone marijuana, but I figure Ben knows what he's talking about. He strikes a match and lights the cigarette. It takes him a few puffs to get it going, and then he holds it out to me.

I shake my head.

He blows out the smoke and then takes another long drag. It smells like burning weeds.

Ben leans back against the cinder block wall and then slides down it until he's seated on the mat. I squat down so nothing's touching the floor except my sneakers. He flicks the ash off the cigarette. "I know a kid named Hitler."

"Adolf?"

"No, Ron."

"Ronald Hitler? You're kidding."

He takes another drag, squinting his eyes as he does it. "At this camp I got sent to last summer there was this kid named Ronny Hitler, and the thing is, he was really cool, you know. Not a skinhead or anything."

"I'd like to be named Genghis. Genghis Brown—what do you think?"

"How about Ben the Ripper?"

"Or Devon the Hun?"

A clunking noise scares us to our feet, then turns into a hum. Ben leans back against the wall. "It was just the boiler starting up."

"Maybe we should get out of here before somebody catches us."

He looks at the stub of the joint burning toward his fingertips. "One more drag."

He takes a long hit, and we stay there for a minute, listening to the boiler. It's as if we're underground, and the whole world above us has disappeared. Maybe if we were the last two kids alive on earth, I'd try the marijuana. But seeing his saliva on the end of the cigarette makes me feel sick. It's also a little exciting, though—me, Devon the Straight, Devon the Quiet, Devon the Polite, doing something totally wrong right under the feet of the teachers.

CHAPTER 13

I hate my name. "Devon" sounds like a stuck-up WASP rich kid, which I'm not—at least the stuck-up part. I don't feel rich, either. I'm pretty sure my parents are, though, because they have two jobs and only one kid. They bought a big Colonial house in Belford, which is a fancier town than Amherst, and our new place sits high on "The Hill," as everyone calls it, which is obviously the rich part of town since it looks down on everywhere else.

After school on Friday I went to the Belford Free Library and checked out a book called *How to Change Your Name to Anything You Want*. From what I can figure, I could change my name in Massachusetts for less than a hundred dollars. Of course, Mom and Dad would have to give me permission to do it since I'm not eighteen, and that could be a problem because I'm not thinking of changing to Jeremy or Jesse or Josh or Jason or any other stupid J name. I want something different. *Mozambique* sounds good to me. I like the way it looks in big black letters on the cover of an old *National Geographic* we have at home. Except people would probably just shorten that to Mo or Moe. I could accept Mow as a nickname, but you can't count on people spelling your name like you want. There are other possibilities, such as Sandwich—Sandy for short—or maybe Asphalt, Fur, Soap, Rivet . . .

Dr. W. taps his desk with his pen. "Devon, can I have your attention?"

"Sure, take it. I'm not using it."

"That's very funny."

"Really? I wasn't even trying to be funny. I'm never funny if I try."

"Well, today I'd like to start with a game."

I figure he means Connect Four or Stratego, like I played with Dr. Castelli, but he takes out a deck of cards. "I want you to pick a card and then talk for one minute about the statement written on it."

"Why do I have to do that?"

"Because it's the game."

"You mean I lose if I talk for fifty-five seconds . . . or two minutes?"

"No. There's no winning or losing."

"So it's not really a game."

"Think of it as an exercise."

"That's good, 'cause my dad says I don't get enough of that."

Dr. W. spreads the deck, and I take a card from the middle, exactly between his hands. I turn it over and read to myself: *Imagine you are taking over as principal of your school. What would you do first?* This is easy. "I'd shoot myself."

Dr. W. leans forward to see what's written on my card. I look at my watch. It only took me two seconds to say this. I still have fifty-eight seconds to go. *I'd shoot myself.* That's all I can think of. I hate this game, because why should I have to talk more than I need to? Once you shoot yourself, time stops for you, doesn't it? So why does it keep on going in this stupid game?

Dr. W. looks at *his* watch. "You have a lot of time left."

"I'd shoot myself. Shoot myself. Shoot myself. Shoot myself. Shoot myself."

"Okay, Devon. I get the idea."

Maybe he gets the idea, but my minute isn't over and I'm going to play this game exactly by the rules. "Shoot myself. Shoot myself. Shoot myself. Shoot myself . . ."

My sixty seconds are up. Dr. W. takes the card from me and puts the deck back in his desk. I guess he doesn't want to play this game anymore.

"We haven't talked much about your new school, Devon. How do you like it?"

"It's like regular school, only the kids are smarter."

"How are you doing making friends?"

"I don't know. How many am I supposed to have after a month?"

"There's no set number. Some people have lots of friends, others need just one good friend."

"I don't need friends."

"Do you *want* friends?"

"Yes . . . no . . . I don't think about it."

"Everybody needs friends. You know, studies show that people with friends are healthier and happier, and they . . . "

Here we go with another friends lecture. My father says it's a medical fact that people with lots of friends live longer. I can see the bumper sticker: Friends Help Friends Live Longer. The thing is, I don't care about living longer. Maybe when I'm ready to die I'll care about it, but not now.

"Friends can be very helpful to you, Devon."

"Okay, I've made a friend already. There's this girl I eat lunch with sometimes. I think she likes me."

"That's good. Is there a chance you might ask her out on a date?"

A date? Is he crazy? I don't think Tanya's going to jump from Alonzo to me. "We're not that kind of friends."

"What about boy friends?"

"Boyfriends?"

"Friends who are boys."

"Oh, yeah, I got a kid who's a friend, too. He asked me to do something with him last week during school." What he asked me to do was smoke weed with him, but I'm not going to mention that.

"That's nice. What's he like?"

"I don't know what he likes, the usual stuff, I guess."

"I mean, what *is* he like."

"Oh, he's got purple hair and he wears army boots and he's kind of skinny like me and he calls everybody a Nazi."

"Sounds like a lively boy. How did you meet him?"

"He just started talking to me one day after art. He

probably doesn't have any friends—that's why he came up to me."

"Maybe he has other friends and he just wanted to get to know you in particular."

"Actually, he's probably a loser like me. One loser can always tell another."

Dr. W. stares at me for a while and then stands up and goes to his file cabinet. He pulls out a notebook covered in plastic.

"I like to be clear with my clients as to what my goal is in these sessions, and with you, Devon, it's figuring out what makes you anxious, what compels you to do things . . . eat a certain number of M&Ms, for instance. There could be a chemical imbalance in your brain, or perhaps you've developed a way of interacting with the world based on some experiences early in your childhood. Another possibility is that you have diminished self-esteem—you're not sure how you fit into social situations with people, and so you're always trying little tricks to make sure things go right for you. For now that's the possibility I want to address." He opens the book, and I see it isn't a real book at all. "These are motivational tapes. I'd like you to put them on your tape player as you walk to school, or listen to them in your bedroom. I think you'll find them pretty powerful."

I take the book and run my hand across the smooth, cold plastic. Sure, I can use motivation, but to do what?

The tapes *are* pretty powerful, just like Dr. W. said. What I especially like is that you don't really have to think at all. You just listen.

The first thing I'm learning is that I can do anything I want in life, if I just have enough self-esteem. The man on the tape says, "You, too, will be able to produce miracles." I guess he means getting rid of my tendencies—that would be a miracle.

I've already listened to cassette one, and it's made me hungry. So I go downstairs and help myself to a bowl of Jell-O and a blueberry muffin and a Kudos bar and four Hershey's Kisses and a big glass of Newman's Own Old-Fashioned Roadside Virgin Lemonade, which Mom buys just for me, so I'm allowed to drink it out of the carton. It tastes better than regular lemonade, and I like the name.

It's surprising how simple this self-esteem really is. I always thought you got it from making A's in class, being the star at sports, and other stuff like that. But the tape says that self-esteem isn't about achieving anything—it's what you think about yourself not achieving anything.

All you need to do is think good thoughts about yourself. The way you do that is by getting rid of all the bad thoughts other people are putting into your head about you. The tapes even give you magic words to do this— "Cancel Cancel." When somebody calls me crazy or looks at me like I'm weird, I'm supposed to think to myself: *No matter what you say or do to me, I'm still a good person.* Then I'm to say, "Cancel Cancel," which erases the negative thoughts.

I wonder about that. Why isn't one Cancel enough? And if two Cancels are good, why aren't three better? I bet four would be perfect for me.

■ ■ ■ ■

When Mom comes home from work, she stops by my room and sticks her head in the door. She's holding her large leather briefcase, which means she has work to do tonight.

"How did your session go today, Devon?"

"It went."

She gives me her irritated look.

"It went okay. Dr. Wasserman gave me some motivational tapes, and I've been listening to them. They're pretty powerful."

"What are the tapes supposed to motivate you to do?"

That's what I was wondering. Mom thinks like me sometimes. Or maybe I think like her.

"Get self-esteem. The doc thinks I don't have enough of it."

"Well, I'm glad you're enjoying going to him. Your father should be home soon, and then we'll have dinner."

With that she closes my door, leaving me wondering how she could think I enjoy going to a shrink.

The difficult thing with self-esteem is keeping other people from interfering with it. For instance, when Ms. Hite in English asked this kid Carl to define *antebellum*, he said "beautiful aunt." I thought he was making a joke and laughed. Nobody else did. Everybody looked at me. I felt terrible for laughing at him, especially since he looks kind of like an ostrich. I'm not making fun of him, really—I'm just describing how he looks. Anyway, Ms. Hite gave me the most surprised expression I've ever seen on a teacher. How does she know me well enough to be surprised about something I did? It's only been five weeks. Maybe I'm one of those thoughtless kids who laughs at other people all the time.

Then in gym class Coach got so mad at me for showing up without my Baker shorts and T-shirt again that he threw a ratty old uniform at me and told me to put it on. It looked like it had been worn by a thousand kids who'd forgotten their gym clothes over the years. I picked up the shirt and shorts, and they smelled like ammonia. I walked to the locker room as if I was going to change into them, then just kept going to the nurse's office. I told Mrs. Cahill I felt sick, and she let me lie down on her couch. The room smelled like Bactine. I fell asleep.

After a day like that I need a hit of self-esteem. So I put away my schoolbooks and lock myself in the bathroom with the tapes. Then I strip down to nothing for the Nude Mirror Exercise. With the sink in the way, I can only see the top half of myself, which is good because I don't think I'm ready to try self-esteem on the bottom half of me yet.

I start at the top of my head. How can anyone be born with red hair? It's unnatural. God, I look like a flamer! *Cancel Cancel.* "Okay," I say out loud, because that's what the tape tells me to do. "I'd look pretty lame without any hair at all, wouldn't I? And it is curly—girls like curly hair. There, two positive things about my hair."

With that taken care of, I move on to the other parts of my face. "Ears, I'm sorry you're so small—no, I'm not sorry. I love small ears. They're better than big ears any day. Eyes, I shouldn't wish you were blue. You look great muddy brown or whatever color you are. And crooked teeth, well, obviously you're why I never smile and people think I'm depressed all the time. But that's okay because I *am* pretty depressed most of the time. Ears, eyes, teeth—I love you all!"

I lean over the sink, and even though the tape doesn't

say to do this, I figure I deserve a quick kiss on the lips for being so lovable. Actually, now that I think about it, the lips are the only place you can kiss yourself in a mirror. That's kind of cool.

CHAPTER 14

Tanya and I have gotten our lunch routine down. I talked to her a few times in English before Alonzo showed up for class, and now she comes out on the back steps to eat with me every Monday and Friday. The other days she has clubs or other stuff to do.

Today's Friday, and she's three minutes late. I open my lunch bag and see the four plastic bags—carrots, wafers, M&Ms, and sandwich. I reach in for the wafers—I even open the bag—then put them back. I've never started eating before she came, so if I do this time maybe she won't come. She could be sick, or in trouble. She could have gotten back together with Alonzo. Or maybe I disrespected her again and didn't know it. There's an awful lot to worry about, if you think about it.

"What's up?"

It's Tanya, and she's wearing a yellow jacket with black stripes on the arms, the colors of The Baker Academy.

"Nothing. I was just getting ready to eat."

She sits down next to me, on the left, where I always leave room for her.

"Isn't it hard eating with those gloves on?"

"Not really. I'm used to it, and these aren't very thick gloves."

She wiggles her fingers. "It's not even that cold today."

"I know, but I have this problem with my circulation. My blood's kind of thin, so it doesn't move around my body right, and my hands get really cold."

"Let me feel."

She puts her hands out in the air between us, waiting for me to take off my gloves.

"Well, they wouldn't feel cold to you. It's on the inside they feel cold, to me. So it wouldn't be any use you feeling them."

She stares at me. She has this way of staring that's kind of unnerving. "You don't want me to touch your hands?"

"No, it's not that. It's just that these gloves are really tight 'cause they're made for handball. So they're hard to get on and off."

She knows I'm making this up. She probably even knows that I know that she knows. Still, she isn't calling me a liar or anything.

"Well, maybe someday when you're not wearing your gloves I can feel your hand."

I haven't touched anybody's hand since I used to sit with Granddad when he was sick. His fingers were all twisted up from arthritis, and it was like holding a beer pretzel.

Tanya's hand isn't anything like his. Her fingers are

straight and long. Her nails are bright red. Her hands are as big as mine. I wonder what it would feel like to hold them.

She finishes her ice cream cone. "Food tastes better outside—you ever notice that?"

I never had, but I nod.

She folds up her ice cream wrapper and sticks it in her backpack. "You know what I hate? It's when you're telling something to somebody, and before you're even finished they say, 'Oh yeah, that's like . . .' and then they start telling *you* something. That's annoying."

I could see how that would be annoying, so I nod again. Tanya reaches up to her earring, which looks like a tiny cross, and starts playing with it.

"How come you never ask me to do anything?"

"Like what?"

"Like go to a movie."

"I don't go to movies."

"Why not?"

"It's kind of hard for me to sit still for two hours, you know. I get to thinking about stuff."

"Like what?"

Should I tell her this? I don't want to scare her away. She already knows I eat four of everything for lunch and that I won't take my gloves off. How many more weird things about me can she take knowing?

"I get kind of nervous, that's all."

"Nervous about what?"

This is getting hard. I give her an answer and she comes right back with another question. I don't even have time to think. I eat a wafer.

"Do you really want to know? Because you might think I'm crazy if I tell you."

"I don't mind crazy."

"Okay. Well, in a movie things happen between the actors—that's what most people are looking at. But me, I'll see something in the background, and I'll want to change it. Like inside a house, I'll see the shades on the windows. One of them will be halfway down and the other will be three-quarters down. I'll sit there the whole movie wanting somebody to make them both the same."

"How come?"

"I don't know. I get to thinking something bad's going to happen if they don't. Like maybe there's a dog in the movie. I just know he's going to get run over by a car, unless somebody makes the shades even."

Tanya stretches her legs on the steps, and it surprises me that they reach farther down than mine.

"But the movie has already been made. What's going to happen already happened. You can't change anything."

"Yeah, I know, that's why I don't go to movies."

She shrugs, and I can't tell if that means she understands or doesn't.

Still lifes.

What could be duller than drawing things that don't move? Why not call them "still deads"?

Why does the world go so slow? Why don't flowers grow a foot an hour and stars race across the sky and winds blow like a hurricane every day? Why does it take so long for things to freeze and melt? Why can't people leap like cats instead of creeping along, one dumb foot at a time? I would have made things happen a lot more quickly, if I'd been in charge. God made things pretty boring. I think He created it for adults, not for kids.

I pull out my sketchpad and stare at the bowl of pears and apples and one green banana that Mrs. Cohen has arranged on her desk. I try to will something to happen with this fruit—maybe a worm crawling from the apple, or the banana magically peeling itself, or one of the pears exploding. Then I'd have something to draw.

"Please begin, Devon."

She always stands in the back of the room, where she can see everybody and nobody can see her. I don't like teachers who do that.

Up ahead of me, Ben is sitting at his easel with his arms crossed. He hasn't taken out his pens yet. In a minute Mrs. Cohen will tap him on the shoulder and ask if he's napping, and the class will laugh. Then what will he do? I don't have any idea. It's strange being around someone who might at any moment do absolutely anything. I almost always know what I'm going to do.

I draw in the top and bottom of the bowl and lean back for a better view. It looks like a lopsided Mexican sombrero, so I erase it. Then I try outlining the tops of the fruit, but they end up looking more like mountains than pears and apples. So I erase that.

Mrs. Cohen breathes over my shoulder again. "Having trouble finding inspiration?"

Inspiration over still deads? Is she crazy? I don't want to draw this fruit. I don't even want to look at the pears and apples and banana all tossed together in the bowl. They should be in their own separate bowls. I want to be done with this stupid assignment. I don't even want to start it.

"Actually, Mrs. Cohen, I think I'm finished."

"Finished?" She leans over my sketchpad. The only thing faintly visible are the erased lines. "You haven't drawn anything, Devon."

"It's an imaginary still life. That's a new category of art I read about in the *New York Times*. I think the article was in Monday, but it could have been weeks ago, because my mom keeps the papers around until she reads every story. The article said you can draw something and then erase it and you're done. People pay a lot of money for this in New York."

"I'm done, too." Ben stands up in front and shows his blank sketchpad. "My still life is even more imaginary than Devon's because I didn't draw a thing. What do you think?"

Mrs. Cohen walks to the back of the room again. "I think you two want to flunk."

I can see now it was a mistake to descend into the dirty basement of the school with Ben. Now he thinks we're best buddies. Every time I look around he's bouncing toward me on the balls of his feet. Kids who walk like that look conceited.

"You sure you don't want to do something after school? I live just a couple of blocks from here, on Pleasant Street." He's asking for the third time today. He's standing just a foot away from me and my locker. I can smell cigarettes all over him. *18-26-7. 18-26-7.*

No, I don't want to do something after school with him. What I want is not to be wanted so much. Friends are too much pressure. "Look, you have to stop hanging around me all the time."

"Quiet! Everybody will hear you."

I put my books in my locker and lock it. He's still standing there. "I'm not a very good friend, okay? I'm used to being by myself." I pull down on the lock, and it holds.

"All right, I understand."

Then why isn't he leaving? And why am I being so rotten to him? It's not like I have a whole line of friends waiting to take his place. *18-26-7.* I turn the knob twice to the right, once to the left, then back to the 7.

"Forget something?"

This is exactly what I mean—friends are always asking you questions. I don't like having to explain myself.

"My grammar book."

"It's right there." He points to the middle of the stack of books I'm holding.

"Oh, yeah. I thought I'd put it away."

I shut the locker again, slip the lock through the holes and snap it shut. *18-26-7.*

Ben elbows me in the side. "It was funny with Mrs. Cohen, wasn't it? I mean, first you and then me with imaginary drawings. She'll probably flunk us."

"It's hilarious." I've never come close to flunking anything. I wonder what it would be like to see an F on my report card. A-A-A-A-F. That wouldn't look good. A-A-F-A-A is better, but still: Mom would go crazy.

Ben gives me a little wave, and with that he's gone.

On my way out of the building, I pass the advanced biology room. It looks empty, so I lean my head in. The amphibians poster is still crooked. I can't understand how—

Someone grabs me by the shoulder. I twist around—it's Alonzo.

"You're Devon, right?"

Of course I'm Devon. He must have heard my name called a dozen times in English. I'm sure who he is—why isn't he sure about me?

"Yeah."

"You've been seeing Tanya."

"Seeing her? Sure I *see* her. I'm in her English class. I mean your English class—our class." God, could I sound any more lame?

"You hang out at lunch with her, don't you?"

"Sometimes."

"Well, like, does she say anything about me?"

"Not exactly. We mostly just eat."

"She hasn't said anything?"

"She said you two used to go out."

"*Used to*—yeah, that's the problem. She's not talking about any other guy, is she?"

"No, nobody."

"Good. Okay, well, see you around."

"Yeah, see you, Alonzo."

He leaves through the side door to the buses, and I head for the front door. Then I hear my name shouted down the hall—it's Tanya running up to me.

"Hey Dev, what did Alonzo want?"

"He was asking about you."

"That boy can't take a hint. I haven't even looked at him since Christmas, but I can't shake him."

I watch the door as kids go out. Two, three . . . I could leave now, but I should let Tanya go first. It would be rude not to. I should even open the door for her.

"So, you walking home now?"

"Yes . . . no . . . I mean, I have to get something from my locker first."

"Okay, no problem. I'll see you Monday then."

She opens the door as I turn the other way, heading back to my locker.

CHAPTER 15

When I say I hate having dinner with my parents, I don't mean only because they stare at me and talk while they're eating and put me on the spot with questions. I can stand all that. But sometimes, like tonight, Dad tells us how *his* day is instead of just asking about mine.

"It was a bad one this morning." He shakes his head with his lips squeezed shut—his saddest look. I wonder whether he practices being sad for when he's getting the dead person's relatives to hand over thousands of dollars for a fancy coffin. It seems to me that you can't have a sunny kind of personality and be a funeral director. I don't know, though, whether Dad started out a gloomy person or became one because of dealing with corpses every day.

He passes the bowl of asparagus. There are only three stalks left. Dad just took four pieces himself. I think he did that on purpose. I set the asparagus next to me so I don't have to deal with it right away. Mom bites into her slab of steak. I spear a cherry tomato and aim it at my mouth.

"It was a young girl, not much older than you, Devon."

"What happened to her?" Mom always asks this, and I don't know why. Aren't moms supposed to say, "That's not a good topic for the dinner table, dear." Or, "We're all very interested in your work, but how about telling us a little later so we don't hurl while listening to you?"

Dad leans back on the legs of his chair, something he tells me not to do. "She was driving a little red Camaro, and she slid into the opposite lane on Route 2 out by Lexington where the divider ends. Just about lost her head."

I gag on the tomato and start coughing so hard I have to spit the gooey red mess into my white linen napkin. "God, Dad, do you have to gross everybody out?"

"What's that supposed to mean?"

"It means we shouldn't have to hear about decapitation while we're eating."

He eats a few green beans, chewing slowly, and I think that maybe for the first time in my life I've won an argument with him. But then he takes a sip of ice water and clears his throat. "Taking care of people like this happens to be my work. That's what most families talk about over dinner—their day at work or school. Do you think it's *gross* the way your father makes a living?"

"Yeah, I do." Why would I say that? Sometimes my mouth opens and whatever's in my brain just falls out.

Dad stands up and reaches across the table. He takes my plate loaded with little red potatoes and cherry tomatoes and baby carrots baked in brown sugar the way I like them. He picks up my bread plate with the Crescent roll I've fixed with a thin layer of grape jelly. He takes my bowl of applesauce I've sprinkled with cinnamon.

"I guess you won't be wanting to eat any of this then, will you, since it all comes from my disgusting job?"

Mom makes money, too, and she does the shopping. But I know better than to say that. I hold my lips tight to make sure nothing stupid pops out.

That isn't the end of it. On Saturday morning Dad comes into my bedroom and announces that it's about time I see exactly how he earns a living. Even barely awake I can see the joke—"You make a *living* embalming people?"

"That's right, and today you're going to come see how I do it."

I sit up in bed. The clock says 9:25. "I'll pass."

He yanks the blankets off me. "No, you're not passing. I want you to see up close the kind of work I do."

"Whoa, Dad, you got the wrong son for that."

"Aren't you turning sixteen in a few months?"

"So?"

"Aren't you hoping to start driving right away?"

"Yes."

"Well, if you're planning to drive one of our cars in the next . . . oh, let's say year or so, you'll be outside waiting for me in five minutes."

I think it's unfair that a parent can threaten to take something away that far in the future, but there's nothing I can do about it. It's not like I can vote Dad out of office. "Okay, I'll go, but I need fifteen minutes to get ready, at least."

"I could wake up and be out of the door in two minutes when I was your age. I used to jog two miles every morning before breakfast, rain or shine."

There's a concept—getting out of bed to jog every day. It's hard to believe that Dad and I have any of the same blood running in our veins.

"Mercy Hospital," the sign says. Personally, if I was being rushed in an ambulance to an emergency room, I'd rather see "Expert Doctors' Hospital" on the sign out front, or "Don't You Worry Everything's Going to Be Fine Hospital." Mercy sounds like something you give to somebody dying, like putting them out of their misery with a pillow over their face.

Dad drives us past the main entrance and turns into a narrow driveway marked "Service Only." He weaves past huge green Dumpsters and a broken-down ambulance and mounds of construction dirt. Then he backs the van up tight to an unmarked black door.

We get out, but instead of going in the door, Dad starts off around the building. I have to run a little to catch up, and I wonder, what's the hurry? It's not like the body's going anywhere. I follow him through the main patient entrance, and we go down a long hallway. Dad waves to several people, like nurses and orderlies. He seems to know everyone, which surprises me. How did he meet so many people in the short time that we've lived here?

At the pathology department he signs in, and the receptionist gives him a key tied to a crinkled cardboard square marked "Morgue." Then she nods at me. "Who's your helper today?"

"My son—he's come to learn the business."

"That's nice, a father-son operation."

Right. Devon Brown, Junior Embalmer, who spends all day draining corpses of their blood and then dressing them up for viewing in their caskets. That sounds like me, all right.

We walk past the elevator and take the stairs one flight down. Dad unlocks the outer door to the morgue and then pulls out a box of latex gloves from his jacket pocket. He gives a pair to me, and that calms me a little. I can do a lot of things with gloves on.

He opens the refrigerated vault. I inhale the deepest breath of my life and follow him in. The cold hits me like I've stepped outside in winter without a jacket on. I like cold. Germs don't live long in it.

There are a half-dozen stretchers in the room. On the closest one a white sheet is spread over a long, lumpy form. Dad pushes up the sheet, and I can see feet covered in plastic, like a shrink-wrapped turkey at Christmas. Dad reaches for the tag hanging from the big toe. I lean over to read it with him—"Lawrence R. Keegan."

"Who is he, Dad?"

"He *was* a thirty-nine-year-old man who couldn't stop himself from drinking and driving. He ran over a little boy on a bike last night, and then he rammed himself into a telephone pole."

"A telephone pole can kill you?"

"Anything can kill you, Devon, if you hit it hard enough. All right, let's get going. Which end do you want?"

"Which end of what?"

He points at the body. "The legs are lighter, you take them."

I wish Dad had made it clear beforehand that he wanted me to actually help, not just watch him work. I would definitely have stayed in bed, no matter how many years of driving it cost me.

"Let's go, I don't want to spend all morning in a refrigerator."

I slide my hands under the sheet. Dad counts to three and we lift together.

"Imagine you're carrying a sack of potatoes. That's what I did in the beginning."

I figure I have just about the best imagination of any kid I know, but pretending a human body is potatoes? Besides, how would I know what it's like to carry two hundred pounds of potatoes?

Dad isn't making me watch him prepare the body. He said I could wait in the waiting room. So I'm leaning against the wall between the sofa and a large potted plant. The leaves are mostly yellow, and a few of them have fallen to the floor. It seems strange that he would keep a dying plant in his waiting room. Why not give his visitors something cheery to look at?

I've been waiting an hour so far. I'm trying not to think about Mr. Keegan, who was a person yesterday—probably somebody's father—and now a corpse. Everybody who ever lived has ended up like him, or will someday. Eating four M&Ms every lunch isn't going to save me from becoming a corpse, too. Doing things in fours is stupid. I'm tired of it. I'm not a scared little kid anymore. I'm going to change.

On the other hand . . . there's always the other hand,

isn't there? Just when you think you've got something important settled in your mind, the other hand pops up. For instance, maybe I was born to be obsessive about things—that's me, and how can I change *me*? In classics last week Mr. Green read us a quote from a Roman guy named Manilius. He said, "At birth our death is sealed, and our end consequent upon our beginning." If he was right, then there's no use trying to change. I might as well get used to the way I was born.

There are forty-two holes in one line of one square block in the false ceiling overhead. It took me about ten minutes to count them, and my neck is sore from leaning back for so long. The trick to counting the holes is not to blink. One blink and you lose your place. I had to start over twenty times.

I wonder if Dad ever plays tricks on the bodies. He has them all to himself behind a locked door. He could do whatever he wants to them. Who would know? Does he feel up the women? Does he check out the men?

That's a pretty sick thought. I don't normally think sick thoughts. I guess I'm getting weirded out knowing that just on the other side of the door marked "Private," Dad is sucking the blood out of a guy, then filling him up with formaldehyde or something. What if Dad knew the guy— could he still do it? What if . . . Granddad—did my father work on him?

"Devon?"

Dad's standing in the doorway, wiping his hands on a white towel, one finger at a time. His hands are red, as if they've been soaking in hot water.

"Are you done?"

"I just did the basic plumbing work today. Tomorrow I'll put on the makeup so he'll be fresh for the viewing."

"A viewing? Isn't he all mangled?"

"His body was pretty torn up, but his face doesn't have a scratch. I caught a break on that. But I still have to speak to his wife. She wants him buried in his old navy uniform."

"What's wrong with that?"

"He put on a lot of weight since those days. The jacket's so small I'd have to slit it up the spine to get it on him."

"So? No one would ever know. It's not like he's going to roll over on his stomach or anything."

"No, there's not much chance of that. Still, I want Mr. Keegan to rest easy."

I like that Dad cares about the dead so much. Somebody has to. Actually, I think he prefers being with dead people more than live people. I heard Mom tell him this one time when he was complaining about going to a party with her.

My grandfather was buried in his overalls, the ones he wore working in his garden before his heart got bad. He wrote that in his will to make sure nobody would try to put a suit on him. Granddad knew how to get his way, even after dying.

CHAPTER 16

If it's Wednesday afternoon, I must be at the shrink's. Of course, if I keep my eyes closed like this I could make believe I was anywhere else in the universe I want to be. I've always thought Pluto sounded like an interesting planet. At least it's far away.

"Devon, I'd like to begin."

Okay, back to Earth. If I don't cooperate Dr. W. will call home and get Dad angry at me again and who knows what he'll make me do next. Going to pick up a corpse with him was enough "consequences" for one week. It seemed like a "punishment" to me, but Mom and Dad don't use that word. I think they read in one of those "How to Raise a Perfect Kid" books that "punishment" sounded medieval.

"All right, Doc. I'm ready."

"I want to try something a little different today. Let's talk about memories. What's the first thing you can remember?"

I send my mind backwards to our home in Amherst where we moved after Granddad died, then further back to Intercourse, where he lived with us on the third floor, when he got sick. I was the one who ran things up and down for him. He gave me a dollar a week to do it, which doesn't sound like much, but this wasn't a normal dollar. Each Friday he had me pull out his metal coin box from under his bed, and he gave me a Peace silver dollar from the 1920s. Each one of them is worth about thirty dollars today. He told me not to tell Mom and Dad because they wouldn't like him paying me. He said it was his business who he gave his money to, and he wanted to give it to me.

I don't want to think about him. He was the nicest person in the world to me, and I hope he went to Heaven or someplace else good. I tried to be nice to him, too, but I was pretty young then—eight years old. It's hard being nice all the time when you're just a kid. It's not easy when you're a teenager either. The problem is that what seems perfectly nice to you isn't perfect for adults. I can't explain that.

I grab a soft fuzzy ball from the shrink's shelf and throw it up and down a few times. Then I aim at the hoop hanging over the door. *This shot is for Granddad.* I shoot and miss by a foot. I never should have thought that. I pick up the ball and throw again and miss again. I pick it up again and throw and miss and pick it up and throw and miss . . .

"Devon?"

. . . and pick it up and throw and swish—Devon the Dominator scores again! Granddad's safe.

"I asked you about the first thing you can remember?"

"I know. I was thinking. I don't remember anything first."

"There must be something you can recall from when you were perhaps six years old, or even five or four."

"I only remember general things, like going to school and . . ."

"All right, that's a memory—going to school. What do you remember about it?"

I try to think of something, anything to satisfy Dr. W. "Okay, I remember that my kindergarten teacher smelled like glue. She had big hands and sometimes when she touched you she stuck to you. She had hair on her hands, too, and above her lip, like a mustache. It was pretty disgusting."

"Good, very good."

This doesn't make sense. "Why is it very good that I remember a teacher who has hairy hands and smells like glue? Why would I want my brain filled up with that?"

"It's not what you remember exactly, but that you remember at all. Sometimes people don't remember much because they're trying to block out certain memories, and they forget other things along with them."

"I'm not blocking anything. I just don't remember a lot."

"Let me ask you, were you happy as a little boy?"

Happy? I'm not used to thinking of myself as happy or sad. Mostly I feel not unhappy, which is what Tanya said was the best I could hope for at this point in my life. But that's too complicated to explain to a shrink. It's simpler to claim happiness. "I was definitely happy. I was ecstatic, joyful, eu . . . phonic."

"Euphoric?"

"Yeah, that's it, euphoric. I was euphoric from morning till night."

"You're not euphoric anymore?"

"I think I outgrew it."

"What did you grow into?"

Now that's easy to explain—"Depressed, nervous, sad, dejected, rejected, ejected . . ."

"Ejected?"

"Sure. I got ejected from my advanced biology class."

"Does that bother you?"

No, it doesn't, and I'm not sure why. A few weeks ago I would have painted myself green rather than get kicked out of class. But now I don't care so much. I even went underground with a kid smoking marijuana. I don't know if that's progress or not. Do normal kids think it's the end of the world to get into trouble?

"Devon, I'm getting some signals from you that I want to follow up on."

Signals? What am I, a radio station or something?

"I believe that your fixation on doing certain things is your attempt to apply order to a world in which you feel powerless. You may also frequently doubt yourself about things you would normally feel sure of—turning off the burner on the stove, for instance."

"I only use the microwave, Doc."

"Yes, well, the principle applies throughout your life. The French call it *folie de doute*—the doubting disease. Quite commonly such fixations arise from some unresolved problem that occurred very early in your life. Do you know what I mean?"

How could I when he's speaking French?

"What I'm trying to say is that often children grow up with significant anxieties and compulsions because they underwent a trauma at an early age. For certain young-sters, it's being abused in some way."

Abused, me? What's he talking about? "I wasn't abused."

"Sometimes teenagers or even adults don't realize they were abused."

How could you not know if somebody took a belt to you or tried to touch you? You'd have to be crazy. "I'd know if I was abused."

"All right, I'll accept your answer for now."

"What do you mean, 'for now'?"

"I mean we'll have to revisit the question again, that's all, maybe after you've had a chance to think about it."

"I don't want to think about it."

"Thinking about it bothers you?"

"There is no 'it,' okay? Nothing ever happened to me. Nobody ever touched me. I had a perfectly wonderful, super great childhood."

"I see my questions upset you."

I close my eyes and try to imagine I'm standing on Planet Pluto, looking out into the wide open universe, where nobody ever asks you stupid questions.

CHAPTER 17

Yesterday was Shrink Day, today is the weekly Pep Day at school, tomorrow is Friday, the beginning of another weekend of nothing to do. This is how life goes, one day at a time, one minute at a time, one little heartbeat at a time.

The thing is, I don't know where my life is going. I don't mean whether I'll be a doctor or lawyer or anything like that when I grow up. If I'm going to be anything it will be a vet. I'd rather spend my time with animals than people any day. Animals don't judge you all the time. My dog Lucky used to sleep on my bed, and he didn't mind if I got up to wash my hands in the middle of the night. He didn't bark or look at me like I was crazy. He just yawned and curled himself over my feet again when I climbed back under the covers.

So when I say I don't know where my life is going, I mean whether it's going forward or backwards or anywhere at all. I feel stuck, like I'm in some kind of weird quicksand that isn't pulling me under but won't let me go, either. I keep coming up with more things I have to do to make sure I stay floating.

Like today. I walked to school in the gutter instead of on the sidewalk. The reason is that I did that on Monday because they were working on the sidewalks, and I had a really good day. So Tuesday morning when I left home I thought maybe I'd better walk in the gutter again or something bad would happen to Mom. Maybe she'd piss off some angry husband in one of her divorce cases and he'd wait outside the courthouse and shoot her. Or she'd have an accident driving home—hit a telephone pole or something. I don't know why I started thinking about her just when I left the house, but I did, and then somehow the possible bad thing happening to her got connected in my mind to the gutter. So every day I have to walk in the gutter. I suppose this is what Dr. W. wants to know, but I hate talking about this stuff. It's bad enough thinking crazy things and doing them without having to tell people about them. Besides, he'd probably just ask why it's my mother that I always worry about and not my father, like I have some complex about her.

Maybe it's because Dad hassles me more. He's been on me a lot lately about getting out of the house. He told me that it was a new rule that I had to do something at least one afternoon or evening each weekend. I told him I was too old for rules like that. He said I wasn't. Then he said I also had to join an activity or club at school. I told him that you couldn't just join something in the middle of February, but he said to do it anyway and walked away. Another argument lost.

So I've decided I'll go to Harvard Square again on Saturday and see if the old guy is standing outside C'est Bon with Little Sasha. I'm going to take extra money with me and I may buy the kitten from him. I haven't asked Mom or Dad yet, but they got me a dog, so why not a cat?

For an activity I joined the Latin Club's secret project. No one knows what it is except the members. Mr. Green wouldn't even tell me when I signed up. He said the other students would show me when I came to the meeting next week.

I guess that's improvement—I have plans. And the best thing about them is that they aren't today. It's three p.m. and I'm locking my locker for the last time and—

"Heading home?"

Tanya's standing next to me, swinging her backpack in her hand.

"Yeah, I guess so. You have a club, right?"

"Gay-Straight was canceled today, so I have nothing to do till the late bus."

"You're in Gay-Straight?"

"Sure. I'm treasurer."

"What do they need a treasurer for?"

"We raise money to send to kids who get discriminated against. They need lawyers."

"Oh."

Tanya pokes my arm. "So, I have an hour till the late bus. Why don't you invite me over?"

Over—does she mean what I think she means? I close my lock with a sharp click.

"You live close, right?"

"Not real close. Three blocks."

"That's close. I could come over for a little while."

What can I say? Tanya isn't somebody you can even seem like you're disrespecting and get away with it. "My house is pretty dull."

"That's okay."

"I mean, *really* dull."

"I don't mind."

It's pretty obvious that nothing I can say is going to change her mind. I don't know why, but she wants to come home with me. I have to let her.

We walk down Concord Street and under the train bridge. Tanya is stomping on the edges of ice along the sidewalk, making a crunchy sound. She can walk and stomp the ice and look around at everything and talk nonstop—all at the same time. Me, I'm watching out for Alonzo. We turn up Moore Street past the Japanese restaurant, and I figure we're out of his range. Now I can breathe.

Tanya leans against me a little. "Your parents won't be home, will they?"

"I don't know. They work odd hours. One of them could be."

"So what would they say?"

"About what?"

"Guys don't usually bring girls home unless it's their girlfriend, you know? They might freak, seeing me."

"Because of your lip ring?"

"That's funny. You know what I mean." She touches her face.

"They won't care that you're black."

"African American."

"Sorry, African American. They're pretty liberal."

"Maybe they're liberal about other people, but not when it comes to their own kid. That happens a lot."

"No, they'll like you. They'll be happy I'm bringing anybody home. I could bring home Ben and he could be calling everybody Nazi and they'd say, 'It's nice you're making friends, Devon.' "

"So I'm just *anybody*?"

"No, you're not anybody—I mean, you're somebody, and they'll like you."

Nobody's home.

I can tell because neither of their cars is in the driveway or the garage. Still, when we get inside, I call out for them, pretending they could be there.

Tanya drops her book bag against the hall wall. "Nice place. What do your folks do?"

"Mom's a divorce lawyer. Dad owns a funeral home."

"A funeral home?"

"Yeah, he embalms people for a living. Wait here, okay? I'll only be a minute."

She walks behind me to the stairs. "I want to see your room."

"No . . . I mean, it's nothing special—just a room."

"I still want to see it."

"It's kind of messy."

She looks at me with a little tilt of her head. "*Your* room, messy? I don't believe it."

"I'll be down in a minute, really."

"Is this another thing of yours?"

A thing? I guess it is. Mom says I have "tendencies," now Tanya says I have "things." "It's just that I haven't had anybody in my room."

"Nobody? Ever?"

"Yeah, but it's only been two months since we moved here. The cleaner doesn't even go in."

"How about your parents?"

"Mom does sometimes. Dad usually stays out."

"It's like your personal space, right?"

"Right."

"That's cool—I can relate."

I start up the stairs, but hearing her behind me, I stop and turn around.

"I'll just look from the doorway. I won't even put a toe inside. How's that?"

We go upstairs and I open up my bedroom door. I hang my book bag on the wall hook and then sit at my desk. Usually I turn on my computer and then take a shower while it's booting up. Today I just sit there.

Tanya's standing at the doorway. Only her head is sticking in. "This is like being in a museum where they rope off a room and you can only look in."

"I don't think anybody would want to see my bedroom, Tanya."

"Sure they would. It's the kind of room all parents want their kid to have."

"My dad thinks I keep it too neat. One time back in Amherst he took TV away for a weekend because I had my shirts lined up by their colors in my closet."

"He took away TV for that?"

"Not just for that."

"What else?"

I don't usually talk about this stuff to other kids. Actually, I never talk about this. It's nobody else's business. So why am I now? I'll have to think about that tonight. Right now Tanya's waiting for an answer.

"He didn't like me buttoning my shirts all the way down when I hang them up, that's all. It's no big deal."

"You afraid they're going to fall off if you don't?"

She asks me this seriously, as if there's a logical reason why a fifteen-year-old buttons his shirts on their hangers all the way down. Even I know there's no reason. "I just got in the habit one time, and I kept doing it."

"How'd you get in the habit?"

God, she's worse than Mom with her questions. I just shrug.

"Let me see."

I lean out of the chair and nudge open the closet door with my foot. There are my shirts, two white, four blue, three green, then the plaids, and finally the flannels, all buttoned on their hangers from top to bottom.

Tanya shivers a little and hugs herself. "It's kind of spooky, like in the *Twilight Zone*, you know? . . . *You have now entered a world where every button is buttoned, where every shirt is hung according to its color, where every object has its place.*"

I slip into my own Rod Serling voice: *"In this world, you must line up your shoes under your bed, sharpen every pencil, and make sure all your CDs are in alphabetical order."* When I think of it as the *Twilight Zone*, it does seem spooky, but funny, too.

Tanya isn't laughing. "You do that—line your shoes up under your bed."

"Well, sometimes. Not like every day or anything."

"Oh."

I knew she'd think I'm crazy.

We're sitting on stools in the kitchen on either side of the marble island. I'm drinking cranberry and orange juice, mixed half and half. Tanya's sipping water and telling me about Alonzo.

"He calls me every night at nine o'clock. He doesn't say a thing, just waits till I say hello a couple of times, then hangs up."

"How come he calls if he's just going to hang up?"

"He's checking I'm not out with someone."

"Why did you break up with him, anyway?"

"He was getting all over me, you know? Nothing hardcore, but I'm like, 'Hands off!' He didn't get the message, so I dumped him."

A car pulls in our driveway. I know the sound of the engine.

"It's her . . . my mother."

Tanya pulls lipstick from her pocket and looks into the side of the toaster to put it on. I open the back door and take a bag of groceries from Mom's hands. Then she sees Tanya.

"Oh, Devon, I didn't know you were having company."

"Mom, this is a friend from school. We were just talking."

"Does your friend have a name?"

"Oh yeah, sorry. This is Tanya."

She hops off her stool and puts out her hand. "Hi, Mrs. Brown."

"Hello, Tanya. It's nice to meet one of Devon's friends."

"It's nice to meet his mother, too."

"Thank you." Mom starts unpacking the bag and putting away the soup cans and cereal boxes. "Have you gone to The Academy long, Tanya?"

"Two years. I went to public school first, then I won this scholarship to The Baker."

"That's wonderful. I'm sure your parents are very proud of you."

Parents—should Mom have mentioned them? What if Tanya doesn't have any? Some kids don't. They live with aunts or grandmothers or foster families.

"Oh yeah, they're proud. My dad was like, nobody in this family ever won anything. He couldn't believe it."

"Do you and Devon have classes together?"

"Just English."

Mom keeps asking her questions about school and doesn't stop until she's put away all the food. Then Tanya takes over and asks her what it's like being a lawyer and having people's fates in your hands. Mom pours herself a glass of water and leans over the island as if she's talking to an old friend. I can't believe it. I might as well not even be there.

A half-hour goes by like that. Then Tanya looks at her watch and jumps off her stool. "Sorry, but it's time to head back to the crib. Nice meeting you, Mrs. Brown."

She puts out her hand, and Mom shakes it again. "The crib?"

"Home. The late bus leaves from school in ten minutes. Gotta run."

Tanya puts her fist up between us, and I tap mine to hers. "Later."

"Yeah, later."

When she leaves, Mom gives me a look like she's got a million questions. I just shrug and smile, because I couldn't begin to explain how I made a friend like Tanya.

CHAPTER 18

The next Tuesday Ben comes up to my locker after school and asks me over to his house again. I've been making up excuses for weeks why I couldn't do something with him, and it's getting kind of embarrassing. We both know I'm lying.

I actually do have a real excuse today—my first meeting with the Latin Club. But I found out that their secret project is building a Trojan horse to take to this meeting of other Latin Clubs, and I'm getting kind of nervous about it. What if they're planning to put all the kids inside the thing? I couldn't handle that. So I've got two things I don't want to do right now, and going to Ben's seems less bad.

"Yeah, I'll come over."

He looks at me like I'm playing a joke. "You mean it?"

I lock my locker and tug on the lock. "Sure. Lead on, MacDuff."

"What?"

"Never mind. Let's go."

His house is even closer than mine to the school, but almost in the opposite direction. When we get there, he tells me to wait outside while he goes in for sodas and food. That's worse than me—at least I let Tanya come in my front door. It's kind of cold sitting on the stone wall next to his driveway, and it takes him a long time to come back out. I start thinking that he's playing some stupid joke, letting me freeze out here. He's probably inside laughing at me. I hop off the wall to go when he comes out and hands me a Sprite and a bag of chips.

"Sorry, I had to help my mom. She's kind of sick."

"She have the flu or something?"

"No, she drinks too much and forgets to eat. I had to make her a sandwich."

"Oh." Most kids would lie and say, "Yeah, she has the wicked bad flu." I wonder if Ben tells the truth all the time.

We drink our Sprites and eat chips for a while. I don't know what to say, but that doesn't matter because he does enough talking for both of us, like Tanya. He says he's F-ing a couple of subjects and will probably get kicked out of school, which will make his father in Texas go crazy since he's paying for Baker. The way Ben says this makes me think he's flunking on purpose, but I'm not sure.

Then he pulls a tube from his jacket—Manic Panic New Easy-to-Apply Atomic Turquoise Gel.

"I'm getting kind of tired of purple hair, so I was thinking of trying this. It comes out looking like pond slime. We could both do it—that would really send Mrs. Cohen into orbit."

He's serious. Me with slime green hair. I'd look like Swamp Thing. "No thanks."

"It's not tested on animals, see?" He points to the words on the tube. "Cruelty Free."

"That's great, but my parents would flip out."

"So?"

So. What can you say to a kid who doesn't care if his parents flip out? "Red hair looks odd enough already."

"Yeah, I guess you're right."

He takes a chip and then offers me the last one.

"You want to watch *A Clockwork Orange*? I bought it last week."

"What's that?"

"You don't know *Clockwork Orange*? It's like the best movie ever made."

That doesn't seem right to me. I've seen a lot of movies, and I figure I would have at least heard of the best one ever made. "I guess I could watch a little. It's okay to go in?"

Ben nods. "Mom has her TV on. She won't even hear us if we're quiet."

We go inside and he takes me upstairs to his room, which is the messiest place I've ever seen. There are piles of clothes in one corner and all kinds of sneakers in another. Under the window there are rows of Sprite cans three deep and ten wide. All over the floor are potato chip bags and gum wrappers. His bed is stripped to the mattress and the covers are bunched up at the foot.

"Come on in."

"Maybe I'd better go. It's getting late."

He looks at me like I just told him his dog had died. "It's not even four yet."

"Yeah, but—"

"Just watch a little, okay?"

He turns on the TV and hits the play button, then sits on the bed. "There's room here."

"That's all right. I'll stand. I get tired of sitting all day."

The movie is really weird. There are these English kids who like to bash and stomp people, and I don't know why. At one point the police get hold of the ringleader and strap him to a chair and put dilating drops in his eyes so he has to watch the video they show him, which is more people bashing and stomping. I guess it's some sort of therapy, like if Dr. W. tied me to his vinyl chair all day.

Ben's sitting on his bed with his knees pulled up to his chin, his wet sneakers on the mattress. He stares at the movie like he's had dilating drops put in *his* eyes. Every once in a while he bites his lip or sort of spits. A few times he says, "Watch this" or "This is the best part."

What am I doing here? I don't have a clue.

After about an hour, Ben's mother calls for him and he quickly turns off the TV. Then he leads me down the stairs and out of the house without a word. I think that's rotten that he doesn't answer her, especially since she's sick.

In the driveway he makes a snowball in his bare hands and tosses it at the porch of his house, just missing the front window. I can't tell whether he was trying to hit it or not. Then he blows on his hands. "I hate this place."

His house is pretty depressing. The paint is peeling off

like it's molting, and the post holding up the front porch has big gouges in it, like it's been gnawed by some large animal. I try to find something positive to say. "You've got a big yard."

He gives me a strange look. "I don't mean my place. I hate this whole town."

I've seen a lot of towns, and Belford seems better than most of them. Maybe there's something I don't know about yet. "What don't you like so much?"

He grabs another mound of snow and crushes it between his hands. The water drips through his fingers. "Everybody acts like they're better than you. Everybody tells you what to do. Everybody."

"I hate that, too."

"They're all like Nazis. They think they run the world and can scare you into doing what they want."

I should go home. The sun is going down, and it's getting colder. "Yeah, well, thanks for having me over."

Ben grabs my arm. "Wait, I forgot something at school. Walk back with me, okay?"

"The school? It's closed."

"No, they don't get done with basketball practice until five-thirty, so the gym door's still open. I know a shortcut across the train tracks. It only takes a couple of minutes."

I shouldn't go with him. But something occurs to me— maybe the advanced biology classroom is open. If it is, I could fix the crooked poster. I've been wanting to do that since the first day. Now could be my chance. I wouldn't ever have to think about that stupid poster again.

■ ■ ■ ■

Ben's shortcut means going down a driveway next to a house with a dog barking inside. Then we have to crawl through a hole in a fence.

Night is falling fast, and he starts talking about Nazi teachers again. I'm beginning to think it's a bad idea hanging around a kid who has Nazis on his mind all the time. We walk up a little hill to the tracks, and he drops down and lays on his back between the ties. His head falls over the rail so that his neck is sticking up as if on a guillotine.

I look back and forth into the tunnels of darkness stretching away from me. The train tracks start off parallel, then merge in the distance—the perspective they always teach you in art class. I know we'd hear a train coming in plenty of time, but it still scares me to see him lying on the track. I can see the headline in the paper tomorrow—"Boy Run Over by Train, Friend Stands by and Watches."

"Come on, Ben, let's go."

"In a minute."

"Which way does the next train come from?"

He lifts one finger and points toward Boston. "The five forty-five comes from that way. I think I can feel the vibration."

I look toward the city and see a round white light in the middle of the tracks. "Okay, it's coming."

He doesn't move. The light's getting bigger. I tap him with my foot. "Ben, let's go."

"You really care if I get run over?"

Sure, I care. I wouldn't want to see even a rat get run over by a train. "Yeah, I care, okay? Now get up."

"Nobody's cared before. I don't know a single kid at

Baker who'd lift a finger to stop me from getting run over."

"Well, I'll give you a whole hand. How's that?" I stick out my right hand.

He laughs and grabs it to get to his feet. He brushes a little snow off his jacket, then waves me toward an open spot in the bushes. He pulls back a loose part of the fence, and we slip through to the other side. In a few seconds the train rumbles past, sending a rush of wind over us.

We run down a small hill and start across the icy field toward the gym. Ben is walking stiff-legged, like he's in the army. "This is how I come to school every day. Then I don't have to face the jerks on the front steps."

"How come the kids bother you so much?"

He leans his head back and spits his gum straight up into the air, then ducks out of the way. " 'Cause they know I hate them, that's why."

"Then why don't you stop hating them so much, and maybe they'd leave you alone?"

"They hate me, I hate them. It's a primal thing."

When we get to the gym door, he whispers to be quiet as we go inside. I can hear the showers running on the other side of the locker room wall. Then there's the sound of foot-steps on the walk outside—someone else coming in behind us. Ben pulls my sleeve, and we sneak across the equipment room and out a side door into the main building.

It's spooky with the lights dim and the hallway empty. It doesn't feel like a school without any kids here. Ben leads the way past the library and trophy case to the jani-tor's door. He turns the knob, and it opens. We go down the metal stairs under the school again, and then he stops.

"You left something down here?"

"Not really." He opens his jacket. In his inside pocket is a large can.

"What's that?"

He tosses it to me—"Rust-Oleum Spray Enamel, 16 ounces, Black."

"You going to paint something?"

"*Nazi*—I'm going to tag everywhere somebody's tried to push me around. And I took some squeeze bottles from art to make little swastikas." He reaches into his other pocket and pulls out a handful of different colors.

I've never tagged anything myself, though I've always thought it was an interesting way to express yourself. But *Nazi*? "Are you Jewish?"

He shakes his head as he pulls on a pair of black gloves. It's like he's going to rob a bank or something. "I'm nothing . . . I mean, that's what I believe—nothing."

I'm not sure what I believe, but I know it's a lot more than nothing. If you don't believe in anything, what keeps you from doing just anything you want in the world?

I toss him back the spray paint, and he checks his watch. "We wait a half-hour, till everyone's gone, then we strike."

"We"? What does he mean by that?

CHAPTER 19

"*NAZI!*"

Everywhere you look in the school, it's scrawled and scratched and spray-painted. It's on flags and walls and doors. It's on lockers and chalkboards and clocks.

I can't believe it. I saw Ben spray the trophy case, and that's it. How could he tag the rest of the school just in the time I went to advanced biology to straighten the poster? To tell the truth, I couldn't help fixing a few more things while I was in Mr. Torricelli's room, like the rows of desks that were out of line and the clock that's always three minutes slow. I had to climb up on a chair to reach it, then pry off the cover and move the minute hand. It wasn't easy. None of this stuff should matter to me. I'm not even in that class anymore. Still, just knowing those things were out of whack was bothering me. I took care of everything.

"Can you believe it?"

I turn around, and one of the guys on the basketball team is talking to me. I think he's a senior. "What kind of freak would do this to our school?"

I shrug that I don't know, and he shakes his head. "Must be really messed up." Then he walks away.

I start to go off, too, but I see two girls sitting in front of their lockers crying. I figure some kid must have died, like in a car crash, and I wonder who it was. Then one of the girls moves and I see "Nazi" sprayed across her locker. It amazes me that a word can make everybody so upset.

The gym is overflowing. It feels like a pep rally before a game, except the only sound is the squeaking of sneakers on the basketball court as kids take their seats. I sit on the bottom row of the bleachers, trying to hold on to my space as guys squeeze in the middle.

Headmaster Marion comes in with three assistants following him like bodyguards. He taps the microphone set up on the court and clears his throat.

"This is a sad morning for The Baker Academy. Our school—your school—has a long and proud tradition as a place of learning, free from intolerance and fear and intimidation. In one night of vandalism, that tradition has been scarred."

He pauses here and looks across the rows of students as if considering each one individually. I wonder where Ben's sitting, and does he look guilty?

"For the first time in my twelve years as headmaster, I am embarrassed for this school. I'm ashamed to think that any of you may have done this deed. I assure you, we will not allow this insult to our educational tradition to go unpunished. We will get to the bottom of this."

The way he says this makes me scared. I didn't actually tag anything myself. All I did was go along with someone who did. I wasn't even with him most of the time. But still.

Okay, my alibi is this: *I went in the school with a friend— no, just a kid I know—to get a drink of water. I didn't know what he was going to do. I didn't know he had spray paint. He didn't tell me anything. I didn't spray anything, personally. I was in the advanced biology room straightening the amphibians poster and—no, that sounds lame. What I was actually doing was going to the bathroom. That's the reason I went into the school in the first place . . . and to get a drink of water.*

That's a pretty good defense, I think. But I don't want to have to explain myself, because even though I didn't do anything they could still punish me for just being there. I remember that from civics last year: a person who helps with a crime or even hangs around when a crime is being committed can be considered as guilty as the person who did it.

I don't think that's fair. Whoever wrote that law didn't remember being a kid.

In English, Ms. Hite spends the entire period discussing the rise of the National Socialist Workers' Party in Germany. She explains the subjugation of the Germans after World War I and the nationalism that emerged from their humiliation. She talks of Jews as scapegoats. She describes the horrors of the concentration camps.

It's pretty impressive how she can talk so long on history, which isn't even her subject. Still, I don't like her jumping to a conclusion about the tagging and making it seem worse than it is. So when she asks for anyone's thoughts on the subject, I raise my hand.

"Yes, Mr. Brown?"

"Ms. Hite, how do you know the person who did this stuff is *for* the Nazis? Maybe he's calling *other* people Nazis."

"Is that your theory?"

"No—I mean, I don't have a theory. I was just wondering."

"Of course we can't know what's in the mind of the perpetrator until he steps forward and owns up to his deed, or we catch him."

"Could be a 'her.'" Everybody turns toward Tanya. "Why does everybody assume a guy did this? It's prejudice, that's what I think."

"Yes, Tanya, thank you for reminding us that girls can be hurtful as well as boys."

Ben shows up late for art class. Why would he call attention to himself on this of all days? He's always spouting off about "Nazi this" and "Nazi that"—won't somebody remember and tell on him?

"Should I go for a late slip, Mrs. Co-hen?"

She nods, and he turns on his heels and clicks them. That's something else he should stop doing.

She snaps her fingers. "Wait . . ." I think maybe she's figured it out, she's going to say, "You, Ben Cavendish, you did this, didn't you?" But she doesn't say that. "Just take your seat,

Benjamin. Lateness doesn't seem important to me today."

She sets out the bowl of still deads again, lining it up exactly as it was last week. She's pretty precise about these things, which I like.

Everyone takes out their sketchpad and pens. Nobody says anything. I'm staring at the fruit, hoping this time to see some life in it—and then I do see something. The banana looks odd. From my seat at the far left of the classroom I see a dark black mark on the side. Is the banana rotting? I stand up for a better view.

"What do you see, Devon?"

"I don't know, something black." As I move toward the bowl, Mrs. Cohen comes up behind me. At the desk I squat down so that I'm eye level with the banana. She bends down behind me. We see it at the same time—a finely drawn black swastika.

She makes some weird noise in my ear and falls backwards, knocking over an easel. Ben's the first one to her. He pulls her to her feet. "Are you all right?" He asks her this with such sincerity that I can only marvel at him.

"Quiet, here's the report." Mom turns up the volume on the television. I look up from my English journal assignment—"The Use of Fear to Impose Rule." Dad lowers the newspaper from his face.

"At The Baker Academy, one of the area's most exclusive private schools, administrators and students are today dealing with a disturbing act of vandalism that struck the school overnight. On the scene is Channel 7's Mark Myers. Mark?"

"Well, Kelly, *disturbing* is certainly the right word today as this affluent, liberal school does some soul-searching to explain this . . ."

Mom lets out a gasp as the camera moves inside the school and shows "Nazi" and swastikas scrawled on lockers and flags and walls and doors.

"In all, the vandal or vandals defaced at least twenty-seven spots in the school, from the trophy case in the entranceway to the cafeteria and locker rooms."

Dad folds his newspaper on his lap. "Who was targeted?"

"Mrs. Cohen's door was tagged, and . . ."

"Tagged?"

"Yeah—written on, like with graffiti."

"Is she Jewish?"

"I guess so."

The television reporter moves on to another story, and Mom mutes the sound. "It's horrible. To go to school to teach children and find that one of them put that symbol of hate on your door. Maybe kids today don't understand all the suffering the swastika represents to older people, especially the Jews."

"It wasn't all against Jews, Mom. It was written on lots of kids' lockers who aren't Jewish."

"Then I don't understand it, Devon."

Dad shakes his head. "I don't, either."

And I can't begin to explain it to them.

CHAPTER 20

During the next two days, more "Nazis" and swastikas keep turning up in strange places. The news spreads through the halls. When Mr. Harvey pulls down the world map in his American History to 1945 class, there's the word in big block letters over America. When Coach Duffy empties the bag of basketballs in gym, a swastika is on each one. The lunchroom aides find "Nazi" drawn on the napkins, like a monogram.

Teachers are starting to act afraid. Each time they open a drawer or turn a page, they peek first to make sure "Nazi" doesn't leap out at them. Some kids clap each time it shows up, the kind of kids who cheer anything that bugs their teachers.

I'm scared to go near Ben. He keeps looking at me like he wants to talk, but I turn away every time. I figure they'll catch him soon or later, and I don't want anybody remembering seeing me with him. I even take the upstairs hallway now to get to classes so I won't run into him.

But I have to tell someone. I've never been part of something this wrong before, and I can't keep it to myself. There's only one person I trust.

Tanya's sitting on the steps when I come out for lunch. She's already licked her ice cream below the cone.

"You're late."

"Yeah, I went the long way." I take out the different parts of my lunch and set them on my legs. I decide to start with the carrots today. "You don't get in trouble much, do you, Tanya?"

"Not me. Trouble is trouble." She dips her tongue inside the cone to dig out the ice cream. "Why're you asking?"

"I don't like trouble, either, but I think I'm in it."

"What kind of trouble could you get into?"

I lean over the railing to make sure no little kid is sitting under the stairs. "I was there when the school was tagged."

Tanya laughs out loud, the first time I've seen her do that. "You're kidding."

"No, I really was there. I didn't do anything myself, but I didn't stop the kid who did."

"Ben, right?"

"You know?"

"I was guessing it was him. I put two dollars on him in the pool."

"The pool?"

"Yeah, the guys on the swim team are running a fifty-fifty pool. If you pick who did it, you win half the money."

"Kids are betting on who sprayed the school?"

"Yep, and I saw the sheet—your name isn't even on it. Maybe I should tell them to add you."

"No, wait—you can't do that. They'd figure you knew something."

Tanya gets up.

"Where are you going?"

"I'm not eating with somebody who doesn't trust me."

"I trust you. That's why I told you."

"Then you shouldn't have to worry that I'd give you away."

"Okay."

She sits down next to me again and tears the wrapper farther down her ice cream cone. "All right. Tell me everything."

Dr. W.'s late for our regular Wednesday session. I'm stuck in the waiting room with little kids ripping at magazines and standing on the chairs and spitting paper balls at one another. I hate waiting and I hate wild kids. Where are their parents? How can anybody leave these squirmy little monsters alone?

Three different shrinks stick their heads in the waiting room, and three kids leave. Finally it's just me and one bony kid wearing a red baseball cap. He has little stickum cartoon figures all over his arms. He comes up close to me, and I can smell strawberry gum.

"What's wrong with *you*?" He points his grimy hand at my face.

I lean back as far as I can. "Beat it."

He puts his hands on his hips and comes even closer. "Make me."

I don't react in the slightest. That's self-control. I could grab this kid by his sneakers and swing him upside down until he throws up—but I'd have to touch him, and I'm not going to do that.

I stare at him and count to ten. He stares back. He coughs without covering his mouth, and I can see the air exploding with his germs.

"Get away from me. Now."

"No."

What would scare a little kid? I figure it's what used to scare me. "Okay, then I'm going to have to eat you."

"What?"

"I said, I'm going to have to eat you." I pull out the white handkerchief that I use for opening doors and tuck it under my chin. "I'll eat your eyes first, and then your ears, and then I'll bite off your little nose and spit it down the toilet."

He steps back a little. "No you won't. You're just pretending."

"That's why I'm here, because I eat people." I growl at him, showing my teeth, and lunge forward.

He falls back on the floor. "I'm telling. I'm telling."

"Tell and I'll wait outside your house until your parents fall asleep, and then I'll creep in your window and eat your face off."

"Josh, what's going on?"

Another doctor's standing in the doorway. The boy looks at me, and I smile at him, showing my teeth again.

"We were just . . . just pretending, that's all."

I suppose I was pretending, but it didn't really feel like it. Maybe I'm finally getting in touch with my inner sociopath.

■　■　■　■

I'm alone in the waiting room. The blue hand of the wall clock sweeps around the circle, clicking away each second. At 3:22 and thirty-one seconds, Dr. W. sticks his big head around the doorjamb.

"Come on up, Devon."

He doesn't apologize for being late, which I think is rude. I follow him up the narrow staircase and into his office. I don't feel like standing and I don't feel like leaning, so what am I going to do—float in the air?

Doc pulls out my file folder and starts reading. He clicks his pen in and out as he does this. Click in, click out. Click in, click out. I'm getting very irritated. I used up all of my patience in the waiting room. "Aren't you going to ask me anything?"

He looks up with a surprised expression, as if he'd forgotten what a shrink is supposed to do. "Would you like me to ask you something?"

Oh God, not this stupid conversation. I know it by heart. I'm supposed to say, "That's what I'm here for, isn't it?" and he'll say, "What do you want me to ask you about?" and I'll say, "Why don't you ask me why you're such a moron?" and he'll say, "Do you really think I'm a moron?" Once a shrink starts asking questions like this, he never stops. I learned that from Dr. Castelli.

So I don't say anything. He keeps clicking his pen. It seems to me that people who click their pen while somebody else is trapped listening to it should be put to death in some slow way—like being hit on the head by a ball-peen hammer.

He stops clicking. "Have you thought any more about your earliest memories, Devon?"

"No, was I supposed to?"

"Yes, I did ask you to think about that."

"Oh, sorry, I forgot."

"Well, let me prod your memory. Last time you were telling me about your teacher in kindergarten who smelled like glue, correct?"

"Yes."

"Do you remember anything else from kindergarten—how you interacted with the other children, perhaps?"

I don't remember the other kids at all. I barely remember the glue-smelling teacher. But I do remember Mom taking me by the hand to school. "She used to drag me down the sidewalk."

"Who used to drag you?"

"My mom."

"You didn't want to go to school?"

"I was just walking slowly I think. I had to step on every crack in the sidewalk."

"Why did you have to do that?"

"I don't know, I just did. And she said, 'Step on a crack, break your mother's back.' I asked her if that was really true, and she said yes."

"What did you do then?"

"I jumped up and landed on the next crack with both my feet. I thought I was doing something funny, but she yelled and grabbed her back. She said, 'See, I told you. Now you've broken your mother's back. You have to be good now.' And she walked the rest of the way hunched over."

"Good, Devon, very good. Now try to remember something about your father, maybe something that happened at home."

"Well, I remember sitting on the living room floor of our house in Intercourse playing with these little red blocks that were my granddad's when he was young. I used to build forts out of them. Dad always made me take the forts down at night, so I'd pull apart the bricks and stack them in the box. One night he was angry about something—"

"Do you remember what?"

"I think maybe Grandpa had just moved in, but I'm not sure, and Dad wanted me to go to bed right away. I started taking the fort apart and he yelled at me to just throw everything in the box. I wouldn't do that, so he kicked the fort and made me go to bed."

"How did that make you feel?"

"Like he was going to die."

"Just for kicking over your fort?"

"Not Dad—Granddad. They were his old bricks."

"What did you do?"

"I stayed awake until I heard them go to bed. Then I sneaked downstairs and stacked the blocks in the box."

"And your granddad didn't die?"

"Not then he didn't, no. I saved him that time."

CHAPTER 21

I can't believe this is happening to me.

Two cops—one big, one small—are walking up the driveway. The doorbell rings, and I run upstairs to my room. This can't be good news. They must have found out about Ben and he told on me. I hear Mom open the door. Then she calls me.

"Devon, are you up there?"

"I'm sleeping, Mom."

"Sleeping? It's five in the afternoon. Come down."

I check myself in the mirror and tuck in my shirt and brush back my hair—God, my ears! They're so small. How could anybody hear out of them?

"Devon?"

I grab my old John Deere cap off the hook in the closet and head downstairs. It was actually Granddad's lucky cap when he was young. It's too big for me and I look pretty stupid in it, but I don't have to look at myself.

Besides, I need all the luck I can get at this moment.

I reach the living room just as my mother is emptying a bag of Pepperidge Farm Milano cookies onto a tray. The cops look over at me. They have guns snapped into their holsters. Why is she giving them cookies?

"Devon, these men want to ask you a few questions."

"Okay."

The small cop points to the sofa. "Why don't you sit down, Devon?"

I don't like that. It's my house. He shouldn't be inviting me to sit in my own house. I sit anyway.

The big cop leans over to take one of the Milanos. He stuffs the whole thing in his mouth, and there's room to spare. "We were just explaining to your mother that we're investigating the graffiti incident last week at the school—you know all about that, don't you?"

"Know all about that"—what does he mean? "I saw the stuff, sure. Everybody saw it."

"We've been talking to a number of people who may have been in or around the school a week ago Tuesday, late afternoon. Can you tell us where you were then?"

"Me?" I know that's a stupid thing to say, but I need time to think ahead, make sure I'm not blurting out the wrong thing. Cops can trap you, if you don't watch yourself.

"Yes, you—Devon."

"Well, I was just around, I guess. I don't go out much, do I, Mom?"

"That's right. He stays very close to home after school."

"Let's say between five and six Tuesday afternoon—that's eight days ago—were you home then?"

"I think so. We ate early that day, didn't we, Mom?"

I look at her and she looks at me with a confusion I've never seen on her face. I can't tell if she's confused about whether we had dinner at that time or about whether to lie for me.

"Last Tuesday . . . I think you came home a little late that day."

"Did I? I don't remember exactly."

The cop pulls a pad and pen from his back pocket. "Were you out with someone, Devon?"

"Oh yeah, I guess I was."

"Who was that?"

I don't want to say. I'm sure they can't force me to—that would be an invasion of my personal privacy and right of association. I learned about that in civics, too. "It was just another kid, it doesn't matter."

"You let us judge that, okay?"

They're cops, not judges. They shouldn't be judging anything.

"Devon, please tell the policeman whom you were with after school last Tuesday."

"I was just hanging out, Mom, that's all."

"Was it Tanya?"

"No, it wasn't Tanya."

The big cop reaches for another cookie. He bites off half of it and grinds it between his teeth. It sounds like he's chewing tinfoil. I'll confess to anything if he just stops chewing like that.

"Let me tell you, son . . ."

Oh God, he's not done chewing and now he's talking. I can't look at him. I can't listen.

"Devon?"

"Yes."

"Someone reported seeing you go inside the locker room of the school just before dark Tuesday afternoon."

"Tuesday yesterday?"

"Tuesday a week ago, Devon."

Mom sits up on the edge of the chair. The cops are on either side of me. I'm cornered. "How can they say it was me if it was dark?"

"Just *before* dark. The witness reported seeing a boy with red hair go in."

"Lots of kids have red hair."

"Lots of kids?"

"Some kids."

"Well, the witness reported a boy with red hair who he thought was new this year at The Baker."

"Oh no, Devon . . . you *are* involved in this?"

She thinks I've done something terrible. I hate that. I'm not a kid who does terrible things. I can't even think terrible things without feeling guilty. I only saw somebody do something wrong. It's not like I watched Ben kill somebody. I wouldn't do that. I'd have stopped him. But this was different. I have to make her understand.

"Okay, Mom. I was there, but I didn't do anything."

The cops nod at each other like they knew it all along. "You better come with us, Devon. We have some more talking to do."

Mom jumps to her feet. "You're not arresting him?"

"No, we're asking Devon to voluntarily come down to the station and answer some questions."

I shouldn't have to answer questions. I know my rights. Mom's a lawyer—she'll tell them.

"Of course he'll answer questions." Then she grabs my hand so hard I think she'll never let go.

There's nothing more embarrassing than sitting in the back of a police car with your mother. She won't stop holding my hand. I try to slink down in the seat, but she taps my leg to sit up.

It's only a five-minute drive to the station. The cops take us inside to a big room that looks like an office. There aren't any bars on the windows. The door is wide open.

The big cop disappears. The small cop takes off his hat and sits behind a desk and pulls out a pad. Then he starts with the questions:

"Please spell your name."

"D-E-V-O-N-B-R-O-W-N."

"Fine, now Devon, you're a student at The Baker Academy?"

"Yes, tenth grade."

"And how long have you been going there?"

"About two months. Not quite."

"So you started at the beginning of the January term?"

"Yes."

"Okay, now on the night of February 22, that's Tuesday of last week, where were you at about five p.m.?"

"Going inside the door of the locker room at the school."

"Why were you going inside the school at that time?"

"I was going in to . . . get a drink of water."

"Were you alone?"

"No."

"Who was with you?"

"I can't say."

"You mean you won't say?"

"Okay, I won't say."

Mom grabs my wrist. "Devon, tell him who was with you."

"I can't."

"Why not? Are you afraid the other person will do something to you?"

That sounds good to me, but it's not the real reason, and I don't want to lie. "I just can't, that's all."

The cop nods as if he's heard it all before. "All right, what did you do inside the school?"

"Nothing, I just looked around . . . walked around. Oh yeah, I had to take a . . . I mean use the boys' room."

"Now, I want you to think carefully about your answer: Did you spray graffiti on the walls and lockers and other parts of the school?"

I don't need to think carefully. I don't need to think at all. "No, I didn't."

"Did you see someone else spray the graffiti?"

"Yes, sort of."

"Sort of?"

"I saw this person spray a little."

"And you didn't stop him?"

"I didn't say it was a him."

"You didn't stop this person?"

"No."

"You didn't leave the building?"

"Not right away."

"You didn't report him or her to the headmaster or any of your teachers the next day?"

"No."

"And you won't tell us now who it was?"

"No—I mean yes, I won't tell you."

The cop gets up and leaves the room.

"Oh, Devon."

I can't look at Mom because I know the expression on her face. I'm always disappointing her—every time I eat four of something, every time I wash my hands, every time I refold the clothes in my drawers. You'd think I'd get used to seeing disappointment on her face, but I never do.

She takes a tissue from her pocketbook and wipes under her eyes. "How could you do this?"

"Mom, weren't you listening? I said I didn't do it—the other kid did."

The cop comes back and sits down again. He picks up his pen. "Now, you admit you were at the school the night the graffiti was sprayed?"

"Yes."

"And we have a witness who saw you go in the locker room—you and only you."

Goose bumps break out on my arms. My face starts to burn. They're going to try to pin the whole thing on me.

"You say there was another person, Devon, but you won't tell us his or her name. Why should we believe there was someone else in the school that afternoon who committed all of the vandalism?"

"Because I told you, and I don't lie."

Mom leans forward between us. "Devon *is* very honest."

The cop shakes his head. "Even honest kids make mistakes, Mrs. Brown. I'm afraid that's the truth."

CHAPTER 22

Dad comes through the door at six p.m. as usual, shouts "I'm home," then veers into the living room to turn on the television. He likes to see the news before eating. Mom rushes in from the kitchen and turns the TV off. "No news tonight. I mean, dinner's ready, so let's skip the news."

"Dinner's ready?"

"Yes, barbecue chicken—your favorite."

So we sit and eat. Of course, I know what's coming.

Dad forks up a piece of chicken. "How was school today, Devon?"

"Okay."

Mom shoots me a look. I'm supposed to say more.

"I got a B+ in my algebra quiz, and I handed in my story for English—it was six pages, which is double what it had to be. And I think I'm going to climb the rope in gym on Friday. I really will."

Dad spoons rice onto his plate. "Just remember to use your legs. Climbing is all in the legs, not the arms."

"I'll remember, Dad."

"Well, I had a sad one this afternoon."

Now I know all hope is lost that he has come home in a cheery mood. It was stupid to expect it—embalmers don't have happy days at work. "It was a seven-year-old girl. She had leukemia. It broke my heart to work on her."

Mom jumps in and changes the subject. She talks of going into Boston Saturday. She says it would be a family outing, like we used to do back in Amherst.

The meal goes fast. I try very hard to eat everything right. When I see there are just three turnips left on my plate, I don't panic. I just cut one turnip in half, and now there are four.

Mom brings in apple crisp for dessert, with vanilla ice cream. She says it's nice to eat early and Dad says it's nice to watch the local news, too. Mom says there's never anything new under the sun anyway, then laughs like she said something funny.

I clear the dishes and load the washer. Mom tells me to go up to my room while she breaks the news gently to Dad. I wonder how she plans to do that. *Now Frank, the strangest thing happened today when I picked up your suit at the cleaners—your pants were missing! On my way home I saw a wild turkey crossing the road—can you imagine that? And oh, I almost forgot, the police questioned your son about spraying "Nazi" all over the walls of the school.*

In my room I sit on the floor, lining up my sneakers and shoes under the bed. I have only four pairs—three of them sneakers, one hard shoes. I know some kids who have twenty pairs. I guess they do a lot more running around than I do.

It's quiet downstairs. I figure the longer the conversation goes, the better. Mom's good at talking, which is why she's a lawyer. She almost always gets her way with Dad. I'd say she runs the house pretty much, at least—

"Devon! Come down here!"

I jump to my feet, but before I can go anywhere I hear Dad running up the stairs, and he throws open my door. "I can't believe it—you did this?"

"No, Dad, let me tell you what happened."

"We've tried very hard with you, Devon."

"I know, you've been great."

"You have all your little ways of doing things—we don't interfere most of the time, do we?"

"No, Dad."

"You'd drive some parents crazy, I'll tell you that."

"Most parents, probably."

"Yes, most parents. But we've tried to be understanding. When things got out of hand in Intercourse and Amherst, we moved. That was for your sake. Do you realize that?"

"Yes."

"We moved to give you a chance in a new environment with another psychologist who's experienced with this kind of problem. We paid for you to go to a great private school where the kids might be a little more understanding, and now you do this. What was going through that crazy head of yours?"

"I don't know what was in my crazy head, I—" Wait a minute, why am I apologizing? I didn't do it. "Dad, listen . . ."

"No, I'm done listening. It's time for you to listen for a change."

"But . . ."

"Be quiet before I really lose it."

I wait until he takes a few deep breaths to calm himself and then blurt it out—"I really didn't do it."

"You have the nerve to say that? You were seen, Devon!"

I'm starting to feel really weird. I remember my self-esteem tapes—*Whatever you say or do, I'm still a good person. Whatever you say or do* . . . Dad keeps ranting on and jabbing his finger in the air. Why doesn't he believe I didn't do it? I need some space to think about this. "Dad, I'd like to be left alone now."

"You would, would you?"

"Yes, it's my room."

"*Your* room? Your room is in my house. That makes it my room, understand?"

No, I don't understand anything that's going on. I just want him to go away and calm down and then later I can explain everything, and he'd see that I didn't do anything except try to be friends with a weird kid. It's their fault, really, and Dr. Wasserman's, for bugging me about making friends. I'd never get into trouble if I could just stay home.

Dad pulls up my comforter on the side and leans down to look under my bed. "You still line up your shoes."

"Yes."

He opens up my closet door. "You still button every shirt."

"Yes."

He opens the top drawer of my bureau. I don't think he

should be able to do that without asking. "You're folding your boxers now, your socks, your T-shirts . . ."

"Yes, yes, yes."

He nods in a way that scares me, like I've just confirmed something bad he always knew.

CHAPTER 23

The headmaster wants an explanation. And an apology. He says that's the least that's required to resolve the situation.

He's pacing his office, which is so small he can take only five steps before he has to turn around. Each time he reaches the window and whirls about, his hand almost knocks into the picture on the sill of his big happy family—three perfect kids and two perfect dogs and one perfect wife. What would happen then? What if the glass breaks and flies up to his neck and slices his jugular? What if he starts spurting blood on everybody? It could happen, and would that be my fault, too?

Dad taps my knee. "Devon, answer Dr. Marion."

"Okay." The thing is, I don't remember what he asked. Something about why, I think. "Sorry, can you repeat the question?"

Everybody sighs—Dad, Mom, even the headmaster.

"The question is simple, Devon: Why did you deface this institution with such hateful words and symbols?"

I can't believe I have to say this for the hundredth time: "I didn't deface anything. I didn't spray anything. Does everybody understand that now? 'Cause I'm not going to say it again."

The headmaster throws up his hands. Dad shifts his chair away from me.

Mom leans toward me. She's the only one still talking to me, I guess. "I'm trying to believe you, Devon. But if I do, it would really let me down if I found out later that you were lying. I'd be devastated. So look at me now."

It's easy looking at her. She has the nicest brown eyes and the friendliest cheeks of any mother I've ever seen. I don't feel perverted for thinking that, either.

"I'm asking you, did you spray the school with that word?"

That word? She can't even say "Nazi."

"No, Mom, I didn't. I was in the school, like I said, but I didn't spray anything, not one single word."

She smiles at me and I feel wonderful because she believes me.

A half-hour later, the headmaster still doesn't. He keeps talking about "the preponderance of the evidence" and "the plain facts" and "common sense."

What preponderance? What facts? Whose sense? There was just one kid who saw me go in the school, and how reliable could he be since he didn't even see Ben?

The headmaster smacks his lips, which sounds disgusting. I'd like to tape his mouth shut. He whirls again at the end of the room. "I've considered expulsion, but that would just open up a legal can of worms that I don't want to get into."

A legal can of worms? What's that? Why not a can of legal worms?

"So I've decided on a two-week suspension. I also expect you, Devon, to pay restitution for the cleaning service we used to remove the spray paint. Finally, you must write an apology to the student body, which will be printed in *The Banner*. Do you have any questions?"

I have plenty of questions: How can you punish someone when you can't prove he did anything wrong? How can you force him to pay for what somebody else did? How can you embarrass him in front of the whole school where he just started?

Dad stands up and shakes the headmaster's hand. "I think that's very fair, given the situation, and I'm sure Devon feels the same way." Then he turns to me. "Don't you?"

No. They don't know what happened. They just think they do. Adults always think they know.

"Devon?"

"Okay, it's very, very, very, very fair."

Nobody speaks on the way home. It's only a few blocks' drive, but still, somebody should say something. It's not like we're coming from a funeral. So I lean forward in the back seat of the Camry into that little space between them. "Have you ever tried tickling yourself, Mom?"

She shakes her head.

"How about you, Dad?"

He grunts, which I take as a no.

There—they've both responded, sort of. The next step is to get them actually talking. "Well, you can't tickle yourself. It's impossible. And they just found out the reason."

Dad turns a corner. "Don't say 'they'. If you're going to relate something that someone said, say whom you are talking about."

"Okay, well I don't know his name, but it was a scientist, probably a tickling expert. I think he was from Sweden, and he did a study with the brains of people and found out that a part of the brain lights up when somebody else tickles you because you're worried he'll never stop. So the reason you can't tickle yourself is because you know it's you and you know you'll stop."

We're home. Dad steers into the driveway of our house and shuts off the car. "I don't think we'll be doing any tickling tonight."

"Right, Dad. No tickling for us anymore, but I just thought you'd like to know."

I'm trying hard to be a good son. I made my special stuffed mushrooms for dinner, which is actually the only thing I know how to make. Granddad taught me. I set the table and poured the water glasses. I even uncorked a bottle of chardonnay and took Dad a glass in the living room. I know it makes me look guilty being so good, and the strange thing is that I feel guilty. I did go in the school, after all. I saw Ben write "Nazi" on the trophy case. I could have told him to stop. I could have turned him in. I didn't do either and I'm not sure why.

Dad isn't eating any of my mushrooms. He usually takes just one on his plate, eats it, and then says, "What the heck?" and takes three or four more.

I pick up the plate and hold it across the table, but he shakes his head. "No fungus tonight, Pop?"

"I'm watching my cholesterol. You see enough people dying from clogged arteries like I do, you start paying attention to what you eat."

I offer them to Mom, but she shakes her head. "I've already had two."

So I dump the rest of the mushrooms on my plate and start eating. I don't stop until I devour every one, and I don't even count them.

After dinner Dad turns on the late news and I stay down in the living room with him rather than going to my room as usual. I figure I should show my face.

Then I get the great idea to do sit-ups. Dad loves exercise, especially for me. So I hit the floor and start doing crunches like he showed me one time, with my knees up and my hands behind my neck, holding my head. I count off fifteen, and I'm rolling. Then I hear on the news, "At The Baker Academy, the mystery is solved today . . ."

Sixteen, seventeen, eighteen. I keep crunching because I know if I stop they'll say my name and Dad will throw a fit. *Please don't say my name. Please don't say my name . . .*

"School officials here report they have identified the perpetrator of the shocking graffiti that appeared on the walls and doors of this elite private school last week."

I glance at the screen, and there are the same pictures

as before—"Nazi" on the trophy case, "Nazi" on the flag, "Nazi" on the locker.

"The culprit has been described as a tenth-grade boy at the school . . ."

Thirty, thirty-one. *Please don't say my name.*

". . . and we've learned that he has been suspended. The administration is not saying what his motive was for the vandalism, and his identity is also being withheld from the media. But I think you can assume, Kelly, that students here will know who he is. Back to you."

Forty-five, forty-six . . . my stomach is throbbing. It feels like it's going to burst on me, but I won't stop because Dad's watching. Forty-seven, forty-eight, forty-nine, fifty.

I fall back on the floor and take a big breath.

"Pretty good, huh Dad? Bet you didn't think I could do it."

"You're right, I didn't think you could do it."

What's he mean—the crunches or the graffiti? This is terrible, because no matter what I do now, he's going to be thinking about the spray painting. I can't let things go on like this. I take the clicker and shut off the television.

"I was watching that, Devon."

"I know, but listen for a second. I really didn't do the spraying."

He shakes his head and rolls his eyes and turns up his hands. Is there anything else he could do to show he doesn't believe me?

"We've just been through this at your school. I don't have the energy to go over it again."

"But it's the truth. You always want me to tell you the truth."

"How could you have been in the school and not know that this other person you say was there was doing all of this spraying?"

"I was in another room."

"The boys' room?"

"No, I just said that because I didn't want to tell them where I really was."

"Which was?"

"In the advanced biology room, straightening a poster."

"You were straightening a poster?"

"Yeah, the amphibians poster was crooked."

"And while you were straightening this crooked amphibians poster, your friend had enough time to spray 'Nazi' all over the school?"

"No, I mean, I fixed the clock, too, 'cause it's always three minutes slow. And I lined up the desks."

"This was important for you to do?"

I don't know how to answer that. Sure, it was important to me, but Dad hates it when I *have* to do things. "Kind of important. I mean, the other kid had something he wanted to do at the school and asked me to go with him. I thought I was just hanging out with him, like a friend, you know. And then I thought I might as well fix a few things in advanced biology, so that's where I was the whole time."

Dad nods, but I don't think that means he accepts what I'm saying. "So, Devon, none of this would have happened if you didn't feel compelled to go in the school when you shouldn't be there to straighten posters and fix clocks and line up desks."

He's right. My tendencies have gotten me in more of a

mess than I ever dreamed of. I shouldn't have gone with Ben. I knew he was trouble to be around. But when the chance came to make things right in advanced biology, I couldn't resist.

It's time for me to change. It really is. I have to control myself. I'm not kidding this time. Goodbye, Devon the Obsessed, glad to see you go.

CHAPTER 24

"Resist much, obey little."

Walt Whitman said that. Ms. Hite read us some of his poetry in English. She called him one of America's greatest poets.

I don't understand schools. They teach you that Whitman said to resist and Thoreau practiced disobedience and Holden Caulfield broke all the rules in *The Catcher in the Rye,* but then the teachers expect you to obey much and resist little. That doesn't make sense. How come they don't teach us about all of the people who followed the rules, if that's what we're supposed to do?

EnglishAlgebraEarthScienceLunchFreePeriodGym ClassicsDone.

Why am I thinking that? I'm suspended. I don't have to worry about classes.

EnglishAlgebraEarth . . .

Stop it, brain!

I've spent most of my life obeying. That's almost sixteen years of doing what my parents and teachers say. I've been too scared to get in trouble. I'd do my "things," but mostly I could hide them so nobody even knew. You get good at hiding after a while.

Lately, though, I've gotten in big trouble, like Dad said, and all because I couldn't stop myself from going in the school to straighten a stupid amphibians poster. Now I'm kicked out for two weeks.

Dad locked the two televisions in the storage room and took the keyboard to my computer with him to the funeral home. I told him he didn't have to go to all that trouble. If he told me not to use something, I wouldn't. He doesn't trust me anymore.

He also told me not to set one foot outside unless the house was burning down. I'm like one of those criminals sentenced to house arrest. I wonder whether I'd be technically guilty if I set both of my feet outside at the same moment.

I open the back door just to breathe some real air, and it's sunny and pretty warm for the beginning of March. The snow is almost all melted, just small patches left on the ground. I stick one leg outside and half expect an alarm to go off. I wouldn't put it past Dad to rig up some system to catch me. He might even have installed one of those hidden video cameras to watch me.

I close the door and look around the kitchen. I already organized everything in the lazy Susan, putting the soups and other cans on the bottom, then the rices and pastas on the top. The jar of pickles didn't seem like it went on either shelf, so I stuck it in the pantry.

I organized the spice cabinet, alphabetizing all the bottles and little tins so Mom can find what she wants fast. Most of the spices begin with the letter C—chervil, chili powder, chives, cilantro, cinnamon, cloves, coriander, cumin, curry powder. That's strange. Maybe Mom has a thing for spices starting with C.

I also arranged her collection of little wooden animals on the mantel in the living room so that they go from the smallest on the left to the largest on the right. The elephants, lions, giraffes, and the rest used to be all mixed up, like nobody had spent any time thinking about them. I wiped them clean with a wet cloth, too. I think Mom will like that.

Now what? I could read some more Whitman or do my worksheet on plate tectonics to keep up with my courses. That would be doing what the teachers said. But I'm not in the mood to obey. I'm going back to sleep.

I hear a car pull into the driveway and hop out of bed. It's Mom. I was never happier to see her come home. I'd be happy even to see Dad.

I run downstairs and open the door for her. "Hey, how was your day, Momster?"

She used to think it funny when I called her that. She's not laughing now.

"My day?" She sets her briefcase on the hall chair. "My day was . . . exasperating, that's how my day was."

She slips out of her jacket and I grab it to hang up in the closet. "It's other people getting divorced, Mom. You shouldn't take it so hard."

When I turn around she's staring at me. I stay where I am, about six feet from her. "You look like you need a rest. Maybe we should order takeout tonight. I could go in town to get it."

"No, you won't be going anywhere."

That doesn't sound good, but I figure she's just following Dad's rule that I'm grounded except for my shrink appointment on Wednesdays. "Okay, the Japanese place delivers. You love sushi, some of those California rolls. I could order them for you, and Dad could pick them up on his way home."

Her eyes are narrowing. Her lips are squeezed shut, but her jaw's moving—she's grinding her teeth. She takes a step closer to me, and I take a step backwards. "You okay?"

She takes a deep breath. "I believed you."

"Yeah, I know. That was great of you."

"I believed you, and I said I would be devastated if you lied to me."

"Sure, I remember that."

"And you still lied to me?"

Why is she asking this? I'm already being punished, so why do we have to go over everything again? "No, Mom, I didn't lie."

She leans against the stair post. "The headmaster called me at work today. They found the spray can that was used in the vandalism. It was in the trash. The police took the fingerprints off it." She pauses here, as if I'm supposed to know what she means. I don't. "One of the prints matched yours, Devon."

"Mine? That can't be."

"Well, it is."

"How would they know what my fingerprints look like?"

"They got them off a drawing of yours in art class."

I can't believe this. The police can go searching through my things like I'm on the Ten Most Wanted List? What kind of country is this, anyway? Besides, I didn't do the spray painting, so they have to be making it up about finding my fingerprint.

"That's wrong. They're lying. They have to be, because I saw who did it, and it wasn't me."

She looks at me for the longest time, like she's searching for my soul inside. What if I don't have any soul to see? Then what will she think of me? "Say something, will you, Mom?"

"Your prints were on the can, that's all I know."

"That's impossible, it can't . . ." But then a picture flashes in my memory, and I realize that it is very possible. I remember Ben taking the can from his jacket and tossing it to me. I remember holding the can for a few seconds, seeing that it was Rust-Oleum, then giving it back. He was wearing gloves, black ones. "Okay, I remember now, I did hold the can, but I was just looking at it for a few seconds. I didn't use it, I swear I didn't."

She shakes her head. "I thought you always told me the truth. Through everything, I thought I could count on that."

"You can, Mom. Really."

"Devon . . ."

"Listen, I know you don't like my tendencies, all that stupid obsessive stuff. I'm sorry I'm like that. I wish I wasn't, you know, and I'm going to work on it next time with Dr. Wasserman. But I never lied to you about anything. Maybe I've lied about little stuff sometimes—I don't remember

162

every single thing. But on big things, I never lied. And I didn't lie to you about spraying the school."

She reaches down and slips off her shoes. "I'm very tired. I'm going to take a nap."

"That's good. You get some sleep."

She starts up the stairs.

"Mom, you believe me, don't you?"

She stops on a middle step. She doesn't turn around. "No, Devon, I don't."

I think that's the worst thing she has ever said to me.

God, how did things get this messed up? Why did I let some weird kid pull me into a situation like this? I spend almost every minute of my day trying to keep things under my control, so how could I let this happen?

I can't believe Mom doesn't believe me. Mothers are supposed to believe their kids no matter what. Fathers, well, they naturally don't believe anything their sons say because they were sons themselves once and know how it is. But moms are different.

It's so quiet in my room that I can hear my heart. I reach under my T-shirt and feel the beating between my ribs. It's amazing that something as thin as skin is all that protects the human heart. Why don't we have armor, like an armadillo, or a shell, like a turtle? Why did they develop good protection and we're left with skin?

I could use a massive hit of self-esteem right now. I shouldn't have returned the motivational tapes to Dr. W. I sit up in my bed so I can stare at myself in the mirror. My shoulders are slumped forward. My red hair is sticking out like I've been zapped by electricity. My face looks all pasty, like pancake dough. My ears look like little stuck-on pieces of clay. Who would believe a kid like that?

"Cancel Cancel." Looks shouldn't matter when it comes to truth or lying. What matters is whether you have a witness.

Obey little. I have to follow that motto now. Mom's napping and I'm leaving by the garage door. I figure I can run over to Ben's house and drag him back here to confess before Dad comes home and goes ballistic over them finding my fingerprints on the can.

I start out running with a burst of energy. I probably look stupid, but I don't care if anybody sees me. The wind is cold against my face, and it feels good after being inside all day.

It takes me about ten minutes to get to Ben's. He isn't outside skateboarding like I'd hoped. I'll have to knock on the door and maybe meet his mother. What if she's drunk? What would I say to her?

Hi, I'm Devon, I live just a few blocks away on Naples Street, and I go to school with Ben—we take art together and I was just wondering if he's home?

That sounds okay, so I ring the bell. Nobody answers. After a minute I ring again. The door opens in and a little kid is there, like a miniature Ben, without the purple hair. "Is your brother here?"

"Which one?"

"Ben."

The kid closes the door in my face. That's rude. And what does it mean—that Ben isn't home?

The door opens again and Ben is standing there in

shorts and a T-shirt as if it's summer. "Hey, what's up?"

"We have to talk."

"I've been trying to talk to you for the last week at school. You keep running away."

He's right. I was avoiding him, but I thought the reason would be obvious. "I just didn't think we should be seen together, you know?"

He moves back from the door and I walk in. The floor is covered with toys and clothes and papers. It smells like cat piss. It's way too hot for winter.

Ben leads me upstairs to his room and flops down on his bed. "So why do you want to talk to me now?"

"Somebody saw me go in the school with you. Now the cops and my parents and everybody think I did the tagging."

"Somebody saw you?"

"Yeah."

He sits up. "You didn't tell on me?"

Why does he sound surprised? Should I have told on him? "No, I didn't tell."

"How come?"

"It's not like you threatened to kill anybody or anything. You just wrote 'Nazi' on the walls, and they took it the wrong way. They figured somebody had to be really messed up to do it."

Ben laughs. "I am messed up. That's what my shrink says."

"You've got a shrink, too?"

"Sure."

"And he tells you you're messed up?"

"He says I never got over my father running out on the family, and I'm mad at everybody else in the world instead of him." He leans back on his bed with his hands behind his head. "What did your parents say?"

"My mom doesn't trust me anymore. Dad doesn't know yet. He'll go crazy tonight when he hears they found the Rust-Oleum can with my fingerprints on it."

Ben draws his legs back so there's more room on the bed. "You can stay over here, if you want to get away from them."

"That's okay. It's not like they'll beat me or anything. They'll probably just ground me for longer."

"You're grounded now?"

"Yeah."

"Then how come you're here?"

He's got a point. I check my watch. I've been gone twenty minutes. Dad could come home any second. I have to run.

Ben leads me back downstairs. "Thanks—for not turning me in, I mean. You're a real friend." He opens the door and pats me on the back.

Wait a second. I came over for a reason. "Hey, Ben, I was wondering, like, whether you were maybe going to turn yourself in or anything?"

"Turn myself in?" He spits past me onto his porch. "My father would kill me."

"Yeah, my dad's really mad, too. I'm getting blamed for everything."

"I don't mean my dad would get mad—he'd really kill me. One time he jumped on me and almost smothered me. Another time he swung a baseball bat at my head and missed by like an inch. Then when—"

"I've really got to go, Ben. My dad will, well . . . he won't like it if he catches me out."

"Yeah, sure, no problem. And don't worry. Everything's going to turn out fine for you."

I run all the way back, and when I turn the corner in front of our house, there's the van parked in the driveway. I duck behind it and run along the side of the house until I reach the door by the garage. I open it quietly and go in through the washer room. I open that door and flick on the light. Dad!

He's sitting on the sofa in the middle of the basement. He isn't reading or talking on the phone or writing or anything. He's just sitting there.

"I told you not to go out, Devon."

"I know, but I had to because . . ."

"Did the house burn down?"

"No, I went over to . . ."

"Then you weren't supposed to leave, were you?"

"No."

He gives me a little nod and almost seems to smile. I don't like this. Why isn't the old man jumping up and down and pounding the sofa? Why isn't he yelling and calling me irresponsible and untrustworthy and all those other words parents like to use?

"Your mother says your fingerprints were on the can of paint used to spray the walls."

"Yeah, I explained how that was."

"It's proof you did the graffiti, Devon. You'll be lucky if they don't expel you."

"Expel me? But I didn't do it."

"Do you have proof you didn't?"

My proof is Ben. I should turn him in, but what if his father really did kill him then? It would be because of me.

"I've never seen your mother this upset at you, Devon. She hates being lied to more than anything."

"I know."

"Then you have to understand, we're not going to get past this until you start telling the truth."

The truth? That's what I've been telling him. What he wants to hear are lies. This is crazy. I have to lie before they're going to believe me! Well, then, that's what I'll do.

"Okay, Dad, I did it. I went in the freaking school and sprayed 'Nazi' everywhere because . . ." Why would I do that? I can't even think of a good reason. ". . . because I like Nazis, that's it. I mean, how can you not admire Hitler? He had the whole world going there for a few years, didn't he?"

Dad raises his hand. I see it, but I don't know what it's going to do. I watch the hand flash through the air and slap my face.

"You have the gall to make fun of this disgusting behavior of yours?"

I step back from him. My cheek burns. I've never been hit before, never even been spanked, at least that I can remember. Now I know what Ben went through. Maybe they should have whacked me when I started doing weird things and ended it right at the beginning. Maybe it's their fault I'm obsessive. There has to be some reason.

CHAPTER 25

The New Improved Devon Brown walks into his shrink's office as calm as anything. Nothing bothers him, and nothing's going to bother him. He might even sit down in the crummy, sweaty vinyl chair today.

On the other hand, why mess up a perfectly good afternoon by forcing myself to sit? Rome wasn't built in a day, right? Start off small and work up to the big things.

Besides, I can say what I have to say standing up. "So, Dr. W., I'm ready to change."

He takes off his glasses and squints at me, which makes me wonder if he can see better with them on or off. "I'm glad to hear that, Devon. What are you ready to change about yourself?"

He's pretending not to know. The Old Impatient Devon would think something sarcastic about the guy. The New Sunny Devon just plays along.

"I get kind of . . . no, I get *really* obsessed about some stupid little things, like lining up my shoes under my bed, and doing things in fours and straightening crooked posters, and it's interfering with my life. So I'm ready to change. You just need to tell me how."

"I see. And what brings you to this revelation that your life would be improved if you weren't so compulsive about things?"

"I got in trouble at school, for one thing. You know about that. And my parents hate me."

"I'm sure they don't hate you, Devon."

I used the wrong word. Parents aren't supposed to ever hate their kids, although I bet plenty of them do. "All right, they're disappointed in me all the time."

"They may be disappointed that you've had some problems, but . . ."

Enough about them. I want to get to the point, which is me. I wait till he takes a little pause. "So, like, can you give me some pill that will change me?"

"A pill?"

"Yeah. Like kids who can't concentrate get Ritalin. I concentrate too much, right? So what do you have for that?"

"Devon, I don't think you should be looking to a drug as the answer."

"You mean there's nothing to help me?"

"There are medicines, certainly. Luvox, for example, is an antidepressant approved a few years ago for treating children with this disorder."

Me with a *disorder*—that's kind of funny. "What's my disorder called?"

"I think I can say pretty conclusively that you have OCD—obsessive-compulsive disorder. The obsessions are the unwanted thoughts you have—about straightening things, for example. These obsessions cause you anxiety, which you lessen by performing certain ritual behaviors. That's the compulsion part."

"So what does this Luvox do?"

"Luvox acts as a selective serotonin reuptake inhibitor."

That's shrink-talk, which I don't understand.

"Serotonin is a nerve impulse transmitter. Luvox helps balance out the impulses your brain receives so that you can screen them to determine which are important and which aren't. Your screening ability is impaired right now. It's a fairly common problem, actually."

"It is? I've never seen anybody with it."

"Most people haven't seen it in you, either, Devon. About two or three percent of the adult population has some degree of the problem. There's some famous people in this group, too. Do you know of Dr. Johnson?"

"No, we go to Dr. Metz in Cambridge."

"I meant Dr. Samuel Johnson, the English writer who lived in the 1700s. Before he would go through a doorway he would twist once around and then jump over the threshold."

"That's pretty dumb."

"It didn't seem so to him. Lots of people have their little good-luck rituals, but they don't often rise to the level of compulsions. Do you ever watch baseball?"

"Sometimes. My dad has it on a lot in the summer."

"Watch the players when they step up to the plate. They'll spit a certain number of times, or tighten and retighten their batting gloves. They're convinced that doing these things will bring them good luck, and yet every one of them will make an out far more often than getting a hit."

"So all of those guys have OCD?"

"A bit of it, maybe. But it's when the obsessions spread to other areas and prevent a person from carrying on a normal life that we need to treat them."

The obsessions have definitely spread all over my life. I need treatment. "When can I get some of this Luvox?"

Dr. W. writes something on his pad. I hope it's a prescription. "I don't prescribe medicines until I'm sure there's no other way to deal with a condition, Devon, such as through therapy."

"We've been doing therapy for two months, Doc, and no offense, but I've been getting worse."

"This has been the diagnostic phase, Devon, and now that the nature of your problem is clearer, we can contemplate alternative therapies."

"What kind of therapies?"

"Behavior modification, for example."

"How would you do that?"

"Stimulus desensitization is one proven method. Patients are forced to confront the objects of their obsessions while being prevented from using their rituals to make them feel better. It's called exposure and response-prevention. We trigger a familiar symptom to show that nothing bad will happen."

Clockwork Orange pops into my head. "You mean you'd force me to sit in your chair?"

The doc laughs, so I guess I've said something stupid.

"No, we wouldn't physically make you do anything. That's not how we work."

"Then how would you get me to sit?"

"Encouragement, Devon. You can get someone to do almost anything in the world, with enough encouragement."

I don't understand expulsion. The law says a kid has to go to school, doesn't it? If one place kicks him out, some other place has to take him. When the kid is really bad they send him to reform schools, which I've seen in movies, but I don't know if they exist anymore. Since I'll be sixteen soon, maybe I won't have to go to school at all. But then what would I do all day—work? That doesn't sound very good.

I'm trying to figure this out when Mom calls me downstairs. I figure dinner's ready, but when I get to the kitchen she says there's a can of clam chowder in the pantry if I want it. I've already been making lunch for myself every day, so I can do dinner, too. While I'm stirring up the chowder Dad comes in and refills his glass of Chivas. A few seconds later Mom comes in and opens a bottle of red wine. I don't see any dirty dishes in the sink. There's nothing cooking in the oven or microwave. I guess they're drinking dinner tonight.

"Mom? I was wondering something."

She sips her wine but doesn't ask what I'm wondering.

"If I get expelled from The Academy, where will I go to school?"

She leans against the counter like she'll fall over otherwise. "You'll go in the next town we move to."

I can't believe I heard right. "The next town? What do

you mean? We're moving again? We've only been here a few months. And they might not even expel me."

"Whether they expel you or not, Devon, the word is already getting around that you're the one who put swastikas on the school. I don't think this town is going to accept you for doing that. And how many people do you think will want to do business with me or your father?"

She's making it sound like I've ruined the whole family. That's crazy. "You mean people won't give you their business just because of me?"

She nods.

"But I didn't even do anything."

Mom closes her eyes. "If you say you didn't do it one more time, I think I'm going to ram my head into the wall."

I don't want her to do that, so I don't say anything at all.

The clock on the table next to my bed clicks past midnight. I haven't left my room since taking my bowl to the kitchen after finishing my clam chowder. Dad was sitting in the living room at the time, reading. Mom was curled up in a ball on the floor, doing her back exercises. They didn't glance over when I passed through the hallway. On my way back I peeked in at them. They hadn't moved. They were barely breathing. They looked like wax people, an exhibit in some museum of strange parents. It spooked me to see them like that.

I didn't hear them go to bed, but they must have, because they always come upstairs by eleven. Neither of them knocked on my door or called "Goodnight" to me. Maybe they wished I'd have a bad night.

I'm tired of worrying about what they're thinking

about me. I wish they'd disappear and leave me alone. I don't need parents who won't believe me. I could live by myself. I could work and rent a room somewhere and keep it just like I want. Nobody would be around to watch me eat and straighten my clothes. The beggar in Harvard Square with Little Sasha—I bet he doesn't worry about what anyone thinks of him.

What if they did—disappear, I mean? It could happen. Dad sees people all the time who are flesh and blood one minute, then cold stiffs the next.

I shouldn't have thought that. Think something bad and it could turn out real. Like with Granddad. Once, for a second—no, not even a second, just a little part of a fraction of a second—I wished he didn't live with us. The next day, he was gone. All I meant was that I was tired of running things up to his room all the time and having to be quiet in the house. I should have kept my hand on his heart to make sure he was alive. Why did I take it away?

I can't sleep. What if Mom and Dad did disappear, like in one of those *X-Files* episodes? The house would still be here, I'd be here, but they'd be gone, just as if they'd never lived.

I open my closet and check my shirts. Each one is buttoned from top to bottom. I reach up to the shelf and take down a pile of sweatshirts. I refold them and stack them and put them back.

I sit on my bed again, and I'm facing the faces of the psychos on my wall. Why did I hang them up? Maybe I was warning myself—one false step and look how you'll end up. I flip around on my bed and look at my Escher print on the opposite wall. I imagine myself on the endless staircase, going up or down. Which would it be? That's the illusion. You could walk forever on Escher's steps and not know if you were going up or down. Perhaps you would be doing both at the same time. That'd be cool. Dad bought me the Escher print. There wasn't even any reason, like a birthday or Christmas. He gave it to me one day and said, "You can learn a lot by looking at illusions."

I can't stand it anymore. I have to go to their bedroom to check on them. I jump off my bed and go out in the hall. I walk toward their room on my toes so I won't make any noise. Their door is shut. Why is that? They never closed their door before. I press my mouth to the keyhole. "Mom? Dad?"

No one answers. My hand tightens around the knob and turns it slowly. I push the door open a few inches, then wide enough to step through. In the light from the hallway I can see Dad's face sticking above the covers. I hold my breath. His face looks old and sagging, almost dead. I stare at the eyeballs to see if they're fluttering, which means he's alive and dreaming.

"Devon!"

The eyes burst open. It's like seeing a dead man wake up. I step back and bump into the dresser. Dad throws off his covers and jumps out of bed. I see his hand rising out of the darkness, coming at me like before.

"Dad, it's me, Devon."

"Get out of here!"

This doesn't make sense. Why is he yelling if he knows it's me? "Dad, I just wanted . . ."

"What? Wanted what?"

I can't remember. Why am I here? Why is he so angry at me? "Cancel Cancel."

"Oh my God." Mom wakes up yelling, too.

"Mom, it's me."

"Devon, I told you to leave this room."

"Cancel Cancel."

Dad balls his hands up into fists. "Stop saying that."

I do as I'm told. I obey. I can always say the words to myself, inside my head.

I run down the hall and into my room, slamming the door behind me. I throw myself on the bed and pull the pillows over my head. But then I toss the pillows off so I can hear. They should be coming down the hall any second to say they're sorry for overreacting. They should be realizing right this moment that I was just coming in to talk to them.

Dad always figures the worst. Why couldn't he have just woken up and said, *Yes, Devon, what is it?* He wouldn't have even had to be very nice about it, not like *Devon, aren't you feeling well?* or *Devon, did you have a nightmare?* They used to ask me that a lot back in Amherst when I had nightmares every night. He could have even snapped at me, *Devon, why are you bothering us this late!* That would have been okay. But to wake up and shout at me and make a fist—what kind of father does that?

I'll never get to sleep now. I stand up in the middle of my room. The psychos are staring at me from the wall. I see myself in the mirror over the bureau. It's as if my picture's hanging on the wall with them.

No, they're *really* crazy. I'm just an amateur at it, a fifteen-year-old who happens to keep his things neat. Like my closet. I open the door again. The shirts hang there, each one an inch from the other. I fixed them like that, with two fingers of separation between them. What did this save me from? Nobody else has died in my life since Granddad, but the school may kick me out and my parents hate me and we might have to move again. That's a lot of bad stuff happening.

I remember Tanya seeing my closet for the first time and going into her *Twilight Zone* voice. The shirts look strange to me now, too, like they were hung up by a robot, not a kid. Most of them I don't even wear anymore. I should get them out of my life, give them to Mom for Goodwill. Let someone else hang them up in his closet.

I reach in and start unbuttoning my blue shirt, the one I wore to Granddad's funeral. It's way too small. I don't need it anymore.

"What are you doing? You don't want to give me away, Devon. I was your favorite once."

God, my shirt's talking to me. Maybe I *am* psycho.

"You're not psycho, you just care about things. You empathize. Let me hang in your closet."

No, stop talking to me.

"Put me back, Devon, and I'll make everything okay with your parents."

Shut up shut up.

"Button me up again and put me back, then your problem at school will go away, too."

You're just a shirt. You can't do anything.

"I'm not . . ."

I grab it by the collar and rip. The shirt tears open, and

what's it going to do now—scream? I don't think so. I let the old shirt fall to the floor.

I turn back to my closet and pull out the next one in line, the white button-down I used to wear to church, and rip it open along the seam. Then another shirt, short-sleeved. I dig my nails into it and tear.

The pile of shirts on the floor keeps growing. The sleeves stick out in all directions, like broken arms. I feel my own arms—I'm finally getting some muscle. I'm outgrowing my shirts.

I reach for one of the snow globes on my shelf. It's the one from Arizona, the desert idea of a snowman—just a black hat and carrot floating in water. Dad thought it was the best one he ever brought back to me. I turn around and hurl it at the wall, over the heads of the psychos. It bursts open, splattering the liquid all over their faces.

That felt good. I never knew destruction could be this much fun. I grab two more globes and throw them harder. The water sprays across my room. I pick up a fourth globe—this is perfect, right? I destroy things in fours now! I lift my hand to fire the thing into the wall, and—

"Devon, stop it!"

There's Dad standing in my doorway. Now he comes, when he hears me breaking things. Mom runs up behind him. He holds her back.

"This is what you want, right? I'm making a complete mess of my room."

I flip the fourth globe over my shoulder and then scoop out a handful of the meditation stones from the basket. I toss them in the air and they crack into the floor like miniature explosions. I close my eyes and whip my hands out to the side. I don't care what they hit. I don't care what breaks or bends or falls apart.

Dad's arms wrap around me and stop me from spinning. It feels strange being hugged. I can't remember the last time he held me like this. Why did he stop?

"What are you doing, Devon?"

There's that voice—always demanding to know, know, know. He's the father, why can't he tell me?

I jerk myself away from him. "I'm being normal, see? I can break things like every other kid in the world, and I don't care what happens. Maybe I'll even die tonight just like . . ."

"Just like?"

Granddad. That's what I was going to say.

"Like who, Devon?"

"Him."

"Him?"

Why doesn't Dad know? "Granddad Granddad Grand-dad."

"Granddad?"

"Yes, I killed him."

I can't believe the words I just said. I don't even know what I mean. I didn't shoot him or stab him or suffocate him.

"What are you saying, Devon?"

I sit down on the bed. Dad sits next to me. I can feel his leg against mine. "That last night, when I was reading to him, his eyes closed, and I couldn't tell if he was sleeping or what, so I felt his heart. I couldn't feel a beat, and then I started clicking my fingers. At the fourth click I felt his heart beating again. Four."

"It was just a coincidence. It could have been any number."

"I kept counting and clicking my fingers, and his heart kept beating. Then I fell asleep. When I woke up, he was dead."

"Of course he was dead, Devon. He had a massive heart attack. He was eighty-seven."

Dad thinks he understands, but there's more I have to tell him. "I wished he'd be like that."

Dad twists around to see my face. "Like what?"

Why can't he ever know anything? Why do I always have to say it? I've never told anybody this, not Mom, not my shrinks, not even Tanya. What kind of horrible kid wishes his grandfather dead?

"Like dead."

Mom steps into the room. I had forgotten she was even there. "You wished Granddad dead, Devon?"

"It was just for a second. The day before I wished he didn't live with us because it changed everything in the house, and the only way he'd leave was if he died. That last night, when I couldn't feel his heartbeat, I should have called you. You could have gotten a doctor. They could have saved him."

Dad puts his arm around my shoulder, just like he did at Granddad's funeral when I was supposed to throw a rose on top of his casket. I couldn't do it. Dad took my hand then, and we threw the rose together.

"Everybody has fleeting thoughts like that, Devon. You shouldn't feel ashamed."

I pull away and rub my eyes. My face is wet from tears, and I didn't even know I was crying.

Mom bends down in front of me. She lifts my chin with her fingers. "You weren't responsible, Devon. Granddad was very sick. His heart gave out. Nobody could have saved him." She leans forward and kisses me on the forehead. "Bad things happen sometimes. You can't stop them. You just learn to deal with them."

I'm learning, I guess. At least I have a lot of bad things to practice on.

Mom stands up. "Are you calmed down now?"

"Yes."

"Do you want us to help you clean up your room?"

"No, that's okay, I'll do it."

"Tomorrow we'll talk some more, Devon. Try to get some sleep now."

After they leave I don't clean up anything. The mound of shirts on my floor looks comfortable, so I just lie down there. Outside a gust of wind blows over the house, and the tree branches scrape against my window. The only other sound is the clicking of my clock. I reach under my shirt and feel my heart. For the first time I can remember, it's running faster than one beat a second.

CHAPTER 26

What am I doing here?

I'm staring up at a ceiling, and it seems very far away. I've never woken up on the floor before. I've never slept all night on a pile of clothes. My neck is stiff. My arms are cold. I should have pulled the blanket from my bed.

"Devon, do you hear me? You have a phone call."

Mom's voice is loud, right outside the door. I don't want her to see me like this. She'll think something's really wrong with me. "Just leave the phone in the hall . . . please."

I give her time to leave, then open my door a little, reach out and grab the phone. "Hello?"

"Devon?"

"Yeah."

"It's me, Tanya."

Tanya. The way she says it makes me think it means something beautiful in a foreign language.

"That's good, you're home."

"Why is that good?"

"You're not in jail. Some kids said the cops arrested you. But they just PC'd you, right?"

"What?"

"Turned you over to parental custody."

"I guess that's what happened. I'm suspended for two weeks, and my dad grounded me."

"That's tough. So what are you going to do about it?"

"What can I do?"

"Get Ben to confess."

She makes it sound easy. "I already went over to his house. He didn't say anything about confessing."

"Tell him he's got to or you'll turn him in."

"I can't."

Tanya lets out a long sigh, which sounds like a hiss over the phone. "Why not?"

"I'm probably his only friend in the whole school. And his father will kill him."

"Did you spray anything, Dev?"

"No."

"Did you know he was going to?"

"No."

"Then why should you do time for something you had nothing to do with?"

"You mean you'd turn him in, if it was you?"

"Damn straight. And I'll tell you something else, if he doesn't turn himself in, I'll walk into Marion's office and do it for him."

It's three p.m., and I'm sneaking out of the house again

to go to Ben's. You'd think I'd have learned my lesson. I can't imagine the punishment Dad would put on me this time. What comes after grounding?

But Tanya's right. I shouldn't have to take the rap for something I didn't do. I'm not *that* good friends with Ben.

I get to his house and knock. A woman opens the door. She looks very nice, kind of like a nurse, not at all what I expected from what Ben said about his mother. A little kid is standing at her leg.

"Can I see Ben, please?"

She shakes her head. "He isn't here."

"Do you know when he'll be home?"

She shrugs and rubs the head of the kid. "He went to live with his father in Texas."

Texas. My witness is in Texas?

"He's coming back, isn't he?"

"He'll be going to school down there now."

This is bad. Ben could be gone forever, and I can't prove anything. "Did he happen to say anything before he left?"

"He said he was glad to go, that's all."

I'm going to die Wednesday, May 5, 2060.

That's what deathclock.com says. It's a pretty cheesy Web site, actually. There's a skull with gears whirring behind it—I don't know what that's supposed to mean— and a gravestone inscribed with what else? RIP.

Anyway, Deathclock says I have 1,857,298,500 seconds left in my life, which seems more than enough for a person to do whatever he's going to do, especially if he doesn't have any idea what that is. Maybe I won't be a vet but instead a shrink for teenagers. They could come to my office and do whatever they want the whole session. It would be the one hour of the week when nobody was asking them stupid questions or telling them what to do. That would help kids, having nobody bugging them for an hour.

"Devon?"

It's Dad's voice, in the hall. He's home early. I'm lucky I made it back from Ben's in time.

"Yeah?"

He takes my answer as an invitation to open my door, which it wasn't. I quickly click out of deathclock.com. I don't want him to think I'm thinking about suicide or anything.

"Your headmaster called. He wants us to come right over to the school."

I check my watch. It's four-thirty. "What does he want?"

"I don't know. He called me at work and said for all of us to come over. We're going to pick Mom up on the way. Change into some school clothes, and hurry."

Dad's always telling me what to do like this—"Change!" "Hurry!" Just once in my life I'd like to hear him say "please."

The headmaster isn't smiling like I'd hoped when we walk into his office. This must be more bad news. Maybe they found a bomb in one of the classrooms and they're saying I planted it. Ben doesn't seem like the type of kid who would do that, but I didn't know he would spray the whole school, either.

EnglishAlgebraEarthScienceLunchFreePeriodGymClassicsDone. EnglishAlgebra . . . If I can say this four times, I know everything will be all right. *EnglishAlgebraEarth-ScienceLunch* . . . Lunch—I'd love to go back to school just to eat with Tanya. That's what I miss the most.

"Devon?"

"What, Mom?"

"Take a seat."

Where was I? *LunchFreePeriodGym* . . .

"Mr. and Mrs. Brown, thanks for coming in so quickly."

Mom and Dad nod. What about me? I came over quickly, too. I'd liked to be thanked. *GymClassics* . . .

"I'll get right to the point. Some new information came to us this morning—appeared right before our eyes, you might say. And we've been following up on it for the last few hours. I thought you should see for yourself."

Here it comes—a pipe bomb, an Uzi, a hand grenade. And somehow my fingerprints will turn up on everything.

The headmaster steps up to the chalkboard at the back of his office and hits a button. Down drops a miniature movie screen. The first thing I see is a swastika. Mom gasps—she's been doing that a lot lately. Dad raps his fist on the arm of his chair. This is going to be terrible. *EnglishAlgebra* . . . The screen keeps lowering. There are words on it, sprayed in black—"Benjamin," "fun," "Nazi." The screen stops, and the headmaster reads the whole message out loud: "I sprayed 'Nazi' all over the school, and it's the most fun I ever had at Baker. Benjamin L. Cavendish."

I read the message again myself. I can't believe it—Ben confessed! Something good is happening to me for once, and I didn't have to make it happen.

The headmaster turns to me. He's picking at the sleeve

of his jacket as if there's something on it he can't get off. He looks kind of uncomfortable. Now he knows how I feel almost all day every day.

"As you can see, Devon, apologies are in order."

Apologies—I like the sound of that. So I'm waiting for the actual words, something like *We were rotten and wrong for accusing you of doing such a terrible thing and suspending you and getting your parents mad at you. We'll never be able to make it up to you, but we'll try by letting you cut classes whenever you want and still give you A's.*

But Marion turns to Mom and Dad, as if he's done with me. "You can imagine how surprised I was when I lowered the screen today. Shocked, actually. We had to rethink everything that went on here, and from what we now know it seems Devon didn't do any spraying of the school."

I look over at Mom. After a few seconds she looks back and gives me a smile. It's a sad smile, though, and I figure that's because she feels guilty for not believing me.

The headmaster moves behind his desk. "I'm sorry we put you through this, Mr. and Mrs. Brown. We thought we had proof—I think you'll admit it certainly appeared that your son was guilty."

Go ahead, Mom, give him a lecture about rushing to judgment. You're the lawyer. Maybe we can even sue the school . . . for ruining my reputation—that's it.

"Things didn't look good, you're right."

No, Mom, he was wrong wrong wrong!

Marion rubs the side of his head as if he's got a big headache. "I guess there's a lesson in this for all of us."

Yes there's a lesson: Don't be so sure of yourself. Trust a

kid once in a while. Don't convict him unless you know all of the facts. Even then, check the facts again!

Mom sits forward in her chair. "For all of us? What's the lesson for Devon—that adults have the power to judge and convict and punish, and we'll use that power however we want to?"

All right, Mom!

Marion hits the button that raises the screen, and the graffiti disappears. "Devon did admit he was at the school, Mrs. Brown, and he wouldn't turn in the perpetrator of the vandalism, which is a violation of our honor code. That would have warranted a suspension in and of itself. In light of the circumstances, though, I think he has been punished enough by the suspension. I'm reinstating him to school as of tomorrow."

The headmaster stands up. Mom and Dad stand up, too. Is this over already? They kept me in this office for hours when they thought I sprayed the school, and it's only taken Marion ten minutes to sort-of apologize.

He sticks out his hand, and Dad takes it to shake. "What will happen to this boy Benjamin?" It seems odd to me that this is the only thing he would ask, something about Ben, not me, his own kid.

"He's in Texas now with his father, and I think Ben's going to get the help he needs down there. Mr. Cavendish admitted that he has to reconnect to his son in a more positive way. They're both going into counseling." The headmaster moves toward the office door, and we all do. It's like he's shoving us out. I can't believe it—Ben in counseling with his father. That doesn't sound like getting killed to me.

Mom stops. "Why 'Nazi,' though, Dr. Marion? Why did Benjamin choose that word to spray the school with?"

"That's interesting, actually. There's no evidence he's involved in any neo-Nazi group. Apparently he was calling people Nazis to strike back at them for the tough time he was having at The Academy. Frankly, he was flunking out, and I think this was his parting shot."

Dad turns to me. "Is that your understanding, Devon?"

I nod even though I don't think I understand any of this at all.

Everybody's quiet on the ride home. It seems to me we should be telling jokes and laughing it up. After all, their kid is no longer considered a "Nazi"-spraying wacko—that's something to celebrate. We can get back to my regular life, where we only have to worry about my OCD.

"So, we won't have to move now, right Dad?"

He looks over his shoulder, locks eyes with me for a moment, then looks back to the road. "That's right, son."

Son—it's been years since he's called me that. Maybe he doesn't like thinking he has a son with all kinds of obsessions. I'm not as crazy as I seem. I just have this disorder that the doc is going to get rid of with behavior modification. Actually, he said I'd be curing myself by using my willpower. I don't know how that's going to work, but I'll give it a try.

Mom turns half around in the front seat. "I wish you had told us or the school about this other boy, Devon. You shouldn't protect someone who commits a crime."

"He said his father would kill him, Mom, *really* kill

him. That's why I didn't turn him in. I thought you'd believe me anyway."

She reaches through the opening in the seat to squeeze my arm. "I'm sorry, Devon. I can't explain why I was so ready to accept that you did this. I guess I thought it was just another odd compulsion that had gotten into you. I should have known that you weren't that kind of boy."

There, a real apology. When someone really apologizes, then you can forgive her.

I squeeze her hand back. "That's okay. I might not have believed me, either."

CHAPTER 27

I'm euphoric to be in school today. I wonder how many kids have ever felt that.

I don't even care that kids have been staring at me all morning. One girl said, "What are *you* doing here?" I started to explain, but the bell rang and she left. It sure got around fast that I was guilty of spraying the school. Now that I'm innocent, nobody seems to know.

So I get my lunch from my locker and I'm ready to head outside to my usual spot on the steps to meet Tanya. As we were walking out of English this morning she whispered that she had a surprise for me. I can't imagine what it is. With Tanya, anything seems possible.

I close my lock and pull down once to check it. When I look up, there she is.

"You ready, Dev?"

For some reason I think she means something more

than to go eat. All of a sudden being surprised doesn't seem like so much fun. "I guess."

"Give me your hand."

"What?"

"Your hand, give it to me."

I hold up my right hand. Then her hand, black on the back side and pink on the palm, closes around it. "Let's go."

I start walking with her down the hall. "Go where?"

"We're eating in the cafeteria."

She's got to be kidding. I stop and try to pull away, but she has a good grip on me. "I can't eat in there. I told you that."

"Not only are we going to eat in there, we're buying lunch, you and me." She grabs the lunch bag from my other hand and tosses it in the trash barrel. "We might even sit at a table with other kids."

"No, wait a minute. You hate it, too. It smells rank. You'll probably gag and throw up."

"Just deal. If I can, so can you."

"But think of Alonzo." Alonzo! I whirl around, but there isn't anybody else in the hall. "You have to let go, Tanya. Alonzo's already jealous about you."

"I'm not his property. I'll hold hands with anybody I want."

"But what about me? Don't I get to pick who I hold hands with?"

"You don't like holding hands with me?"

I do like holding her hand. It feels strong and warm, like wearing a tight glove.

"I like it okay, but not . . ."

"Okay?"

"I like it a lot."

"Fine, then let's go in the cafeteria."

Everybody looks up when we walk in. Somebody whistles, and then a couple of kids clap. I keep my head down. If Alonzo's going to kill me, I want it to be a quick chop to the back of my head. I don't want to see it coming.

Tanya sticks her two fingers in her mouth and whistles. "Listen up. Devon has something to say."

Everybody gets quiet. They're all looking at me. Tanya elbows me in the ribs. "Tell them you didn't do it."

"What?"

"You want everybody to keep thinking you sprayed their school?"

"No."

"So tell them you didn't do it."

I've never spoken to this many people at one time before. What if my voice cracks?

"I just want to say that I didn't spray the school. The headmaster knows that now, which is why he let me come back. I was in the building when the spraying happened, but I didn't do anything myself. I didn't even know the other kid was going to, and I'm sorry I didn't stop him. I guess that's all."

Nobody says anything. I don't know what I expect—*Three cheers for Devon: Hurrah! Hurrah! Hurrah!* Not likely. No one even claps for how brave I must be to make a speech like this. After a few seconds the kids go back to eating and talking to each other like normal. I guess that's good.

"There, that's taken care of. Now let's eat." Tanya pulls me to the food line. The sign over the entree section says

"Meatloaf." That has to be the single most disgusting thing a school could offer.

She taps on the glass to get the server's attention. "We'll take two, please, with gravy."

"Wait, I'm a vegetarian, remember?"

"Okay, he'll have the fish."

The woman hands over the meatloaf to Tanya, then gives me a big plate of some gelatin-looking kind of white fish. Next to it are a few dried-out string beans and a ball of mashed potatoes, made with an ice cream scoop. This isn't going to be easy. At least there's a roll, and two pats of butter.

When we reach the ice cream cooler, Tanya opens the top and looks in. The vanilla cones are piled on top of one another. There must be twenty of them. She digs her hand through the vanillas and pulls out one from the bottom— chocolate.

The cashier looks at it, then Tanya. "That's chocolate, you know."

"Yes, I see that."

"You always buy vanilla, Tanya."

"That's true. I mean, that *was* true. I buy whatever kind I want now."

I grab a chocolate cone for myself and get my money out to pay. The cashier gives me a look like, "I haven't seen you before."

I figure I should explain myself. "I'm new."

"That's nice." She hands me my change, and I follow Tanya to the middle of the cafeteria. She sits at the end of a long table. A couple of freshmen are at the other end, but they don't look up.

I lean forward to smell the fish. You wouldn't really know it was fish if they hadn't put a sign on it. Tanya forks up a piece of her meatloaf and swallows it whole. I figure that's her way of not having to taste it. She cuts off another piece and then stops, her fork halfway to her mouth. "Oh, what a foul and unpleasant odor approaches."

I look over my shoulder, and there's Alonzo coming toward us, with a girl hanging on his arm. "Hey, Tan. What's up?"

"Nothing I can't handle." She sticks the meatloaf in her mouth and swallows.

"That's good." Alonzo reaches over my shoulder and takes the roll from my tray. That was the only thing I was going to eat. He punches me in the arm, but not very hard. "Nice speech you gave there, kid. But I knew all along you didn't do it. You don't have the *cajones*."

I nod that he's right, even though I don't know what he means. It always throws guys off when you agree with them when they're taunting you. Tanya waves her fork in the air. "This boy has all the parts he needs, Alonzo."

"You know that for a fact?"

"I know that for a fact."

I still don't know what they're talking about, and I'm sure not going to ask. They stare each other down for a minute, then he tosses my roll in the air and it splats onto my plate. "Have a nice life together." With that he leaves, the girl still hanging on his arm.

Tanya acts like nothing happened. She starts humming some song—loud humming, like she's in the chorus room.

I lean back in my chair and look up. The flags look colorful hanging from the ceiling. But the Japanese one with the big red circle in the center is twisted up at its base and doesn't hang as far down as the others. Felix should really get a ladder and fix that. I'll have to suggest it to him.

"You're not eating, Devon."

Okay, forget the flag. What's it going to do—fall from the ceiling and suffocate me? That's pretty unlikely. And if it is going to fall, I can't stop it. Mom's right. Bad things happen sometimes, and you can't stop them. But good things happen, too.

Tanya stuffs the last of her meatloaf in her mouth. I pick my roll out of the mashed potatoes and take a few bites. It's pretty soggy. Then I cut apart the fish and spread it around on my plate to make it look like I ate some.

Tanya dives into her ball of mashed potatoes with a spoon. In three mouthfuls she's done. I've never seen a girl eat faster. Then she unwraps her chocolate cone and takes a lick. "Delicious. Best ice cream I've ever had."

I tear the paper off my cone and lick. The chocolate tastes just regular to me, not good or bad. I guess Tanya's using her willpower to convince herself she likes chocolate now.

As we eat our ice cream I look around. In the corner the geeks are whacking at the clocks, playing speed chess. The preppies are calling each other on their cell phones. The jocks are laughing over some stupid bodily noise one of them made. Everything's happening like it always does. Nobody even notices that we're sitting in the middle of them, overcoming our worst fears.

When we're done Tanya leads me to the disposal area,

and we put our trays onto the conveyor belt. She wipes her lips with her napkin and tosses it into the trash bin. "That wasn't so bad, was it?"

I didn't even taste the fish, or the potatoes or the string beans, so what can I say? "The chocolate cone was pretty good." That's looking on the bright side of things.

"I meant the whole experience. We actually ate in the caf and survived. Survival is what it's all about."

Tanya is always saying something is "what it's all about," like respect, or family or survival. Whatever she says seems right to me.

"Half of life is just showing up, Dev. That's what we did today—we showed up."

We head for the door. Other kids are leaving, too. I stop to let her go through first, which is the polite thing for a guy to do. I don't even count what number I am. Four, seven, nine—it's not important. I just ate lunch in a germ swamp, so why would I worry about going through a doorway?

When she sticks her hand out, I grab it, and we walk through together.

epilogue

"Come on in, Devon, I have a surprise for you."

Dr. Wasserman is grinning. It always worries me when a shrink grins at you. I step into his office, and there's an orange chair in the corner where the vinyl one used to be. He waves his hand at it. "It's brand new. Sit."

What am I, a dog? Maybe there haven't been thousands of squirmy asses sitting in this chair, but there's probably been dozens since he got it. "I don't think so."

"It just came today. You'd be the first one to use it."

That's hard to believe. "You haven't had any other patients yet?"

"Not since the chair arrived, so there's no reason for you not to sit, is there?"

I guess there isn't. Except . . ."At the store there were probably all kinds of people trying it out."

He shakes his head. "This one came directly from the factory, wrapped in plastic. It's never been sat on."

I can't think of any reason not to sit down, so I do. The chair feels weird, and it's pretty uncomfortable. But at least I won't have to lean against the wall for the whole session.

"I spoke to your mom, Devon. She said you've had an emotional few days."

I've been slapped and screamed at by my dad. I've been kicked out of school and then put back in again by the headmaster. I've gone from ordering my closet like I'm in the army to throwing all my clothes in a heap on the floor. And I ate in probably the most germ-infested place on earth—a high school cafeteria. "Yeah, it's been pretty emotional lately."

"Well, out of emotion often comes the truth, and I think you hit on it yourself when you were breaking things in your room."

"What truth is that?"

"You tell me."

I ripped up my shirts and then threw the snow globes into the wall. Dad rushed into my room to stop me. He hugged me, and I felt like a little kid again. Is that where the truth was? "I don't know what I said."

"Your mother said you spoke about your grandfather."

Granddad, yes . . . I wished him dead, and he died.

"You've felt responsible all these years for his death, haven't you?"

"Can you feel something and not know it?"

"Certainly. Subconsciously you believed that you wanted him dead and that you let him die by taking your hand away from his heart and not calling for help. Your guilt over this sparked your obsessive thoughts. To deal with them you developed the compulsions to keep your world neat and clean."

It's strange hearing someone explain your life to you. He wasn't around, so what makes him so smart about me? It's like he opened to page thirty-eight of *The Shrink's Guide to Messed-Up Kids,* and there's my picture with a little write-up.

"You just think that's what happened, right? You don't really know."

"It's not just what *I* think, Devon. You're the one who revealed what was going on inside you."

I know myself, that's what he's saying. I guess I'm like an oracle, at least for my own life. Maybe everybody's his own oracle, if he can just read the signs.

"Stand up for a moment, would you?"

I stand up, and the doc comes over to the chair and bends down. He loosens the ties around the legs, then yanks off the orange slipcover. I can't believe what I'm seeing—the black vinyl chair!

"You said this was new, straight from the factory."

"The slipcover is new, Devon. Just arrived today."

"You tricked me."

"Yes, I tricked you. The question is, will you sit in the old chair now that you know the origin of your obsessions?"

It's a good question. Nothing bad happened to me after eating in the cafeteria. Nobody died after I ripped up my shirts and threw them on the floor. In fact, Mom yelled at me to clean them up, which was totally strange. Maybe it is time to sit in the vinyl chair. A hundred dollars could convince me.

"I might sit, if you want to offer some motivation again. It wouldn't cost you a million dollars this time."

"I'm offering something more valuable to you today than money, Devon."

"What's that?"

"A start to a life free of your obsessions."

"Couldn't I have that *and* the money?"

He shakes his head.

Okay, obviously I'm not getting paid to sit in the crummy chair. I have to do it out of my own willpower. I back up to it. *Sit!*

That didn't work. I'm still standing. This is like the first time I dove into a swimming pool, when I was frozen on the diving board. Dad called up to me to close my eyes and think of a friendly face waiting for me in the water. I thought of Granddad then and what he said to me once, "When you're scared just yell out 'Geronimo!' You won't be scared no more."

I close my eyes now, and Tanya's face pops into my mind. *Go on and sit, Devon. There's nothing to worry about.*

"Geronimo!" I'm falling, falling backwards . . . and I hit the black vinyl chair!

"Good, Devon, very good."

I open my eyes and see the doc, not Tanya. I did it. I sat. I proved I could. But there's no reason to stay sitting on this sweaty old cushion, is there? I jump to my feet again.

Doc leans back, like I'm springing at him. "Well, you've taken a big step forward today, Devon, and I think we won't push things any further. I'm letting you go early. Next week we'll take up where we left off."

That sounds good to me. I'm out of there. He swivels in his chair to get something from his bookshelf, and I open his office door. I could step right through. I do it all the time. But I figure, things are going so well, why take the chance of messing them up? I twist around once and then jump over the threshold. Now everything feels right with the world.